"But I like Frankie, too. One's soft and evocative. The other full of spirit and challenge. Just like you."

Frankie glared at him. "I don't like you talking about me like that!"

It was hard to withstand the fire of her eyes but Randall knew what he had to do. "Why not?" he asked quietly, keeping his expression light.

She turned away. "Because I don't!"

"Why not?" he repeated.

The fire in her eyes grew hotter. "Are you naturally obnoxious or are you just practicing? I *didn't* want to see you. I *don't* want to talk to you. Take the hint!"

"I don't take hints very well."

"Tell me about it!"

"I love you, Frankie."

The soft words were received like a bolt of lightning from a clear sky.

She blinked, stunned. "You're mad."

ABOUT THE AUTHOR

A native of Texas, Ginger Chambers now makes
her home in Northern California. Ginger gets
story ideas from a variety of sources. Often she
starts with a specific character, puts the person in
a situation and watches the action evolve. And,
sometimes, the action doesn't stop. *Eagle on the
Wind,* Ginger's latest book, is a spinoff from her
earlier American Romance #395, *Bird in a Mirror.*
Randall Peters, the hero's best friend in *Bird in a
Mirror,* makes another appearance in *Eagle on the
Wind*...now as the hero!

Books by Ginger Chambers
HARLEQUIN AMERICAN ROMANCE

Don't miss any of our special offers. Write to us at the
following address for information on our newest releases.

Harlequin Reader Service
P.O. Box 1397, Buffalo, NY 14240
Canadian address: P.O. Box 603,
Fort Erie, Ont. L2A 5X3

GINGER CHAMBERS

EAGLE ON THE WIND

Harlequin Books

TORONTO • NEW YORK • LONDON
AMSTERDAM • PARIS • SYDNEY • HAMBURG
STOCKHOLM • ATHENS • TOKYO • MILAN

Published October 1991

ISBN 0-373-16411-4

EAGLE ON THE WIND

Chapter One

A cab had never looked so good. A cabbie had never been so welcome. Even the mingled scent of stale cigarette smoke, various humans and an odd metallic grunge was greeted with relief as Randall Peters collapsed into the vastness of the taxi's back seat, his garment bag held defensively to his chest.

To attach such importance to a second suit, several shirts, socks, briefs, a toothbrush and a travel alarm might seem excessive to some, but after the ordeal Randall had been through that day, his behavior was perfectly in order.

"Where to?" the cabbie asked as he hit the timer on the meter.

"Home!" Randall replied with heartfelt relief. Then he quickly added the address before the cabbie could turn to tell him he needed a little more information than *that*.

The act of flying had never been easy for him. A rock hurtling through the air at a speed of six hundred miles an hour and an altitude of thirty thousand feet seemed more than a little ridiculous. And that a person should voluntarily place himself inside that rock and then turn his possessions over to a stranger...

His troubles had started early that morning in Chicago when O'Hare had been paralyzed by inclement weather and all flights were either canceled or delayed, which had caused an unbelievable mess. His flight, of course, had been canceled. It was only after a great deal of wrangling that he'd been able to claim another. Only that flight wasn't booked directly through to his destination; he'd had to make several stops along the way and had changed planes twice before finally touching down in San Francisco ten hours and fifty minutes later, minus his garment bag, which had been whisked out of an overcrowded cabin and placed in the belly of the plane. *Which* plane the flight attendant had neglected to mention. And it had taken another hour after landing to find out.

If it all hadn't been so harrowing, Randall might have laughed. Especially when he thought about the stir he had caused in the Phoenix airport when, after being dumped off one plane for another, his name had turned up missing from the next flight's manifest and he was not allowed to board. And no one in the airport seemed to care except him.

He could see himself as he had been then: ranting and raving like a lunatic, demanding that someone, anyone *do* something. He was lucky the airport officials hadn't called the local funny farm and had him locked away!

A smile broke across Randall's features, which soon increased to a chuckle and then to outright laughter as the situation replayed in his mind. It hadn't been funny at the time, but with the advantage of having finally arrived at his destination, he couldn't help but appreciate the humor.

His laughter continued unabated until he noticed the cabbie's wary glances in the rearview mirror, and he reminded himself that there were funny farms in California, too!

Forcing himself to relax, he drew a deep breath and allowed his garment bag to slide onto the seat next to him. Exhaustion was beginning to take its toll. Even before leaving Chicago, he'd been worn out from the pressures of a three-day consultation in which tension-filled meetings had lasted well into each night. Then to have to suffer such a nightmarish trip home...

To help center his thoughts on something besides the rigors of his journey, Randall switched his gaze to the world outside the taxi. He watched with grateful appreciation as each familiar sight came into view: the lower end of San Francisco Bay, the beautiful golden hills, then Candlestick Park and a little farther on, the pastel crush of houses that clung tenaciously to every speck of available land.

As the cab approached the city proper, it left the elevated section of freeway and slid onto the streets where people from all walks of life were moving busily to and fro. Some were dressed for business, some were in casual attire, some were freezing tourists experiencing their first taste of a San Francisco summer. Panhandlers continued to cadge for a day's hard-won pay.

Randall loved San Francisco. He could imagine living nowhere else. He rejoiced in the diversity of its people and its ideas. But as the cab got held up while a few stragglers from that wide diversity continued to stroll across the street after the light had changed from their favor, his fondness developed a brittle edge. His apartment was near. He could almost see it from where they were. Positioned high atop Russian Hill, it was a place where airline attendants, ticket agents, baggage handlers and assorted passengers, especially crying baby passengers, could be barred entry. A place where *he* was in firm control of his life. No one else.

The cabbie tapped his fingers on the steering wheel and whistled tunelessly beneath his breath as he waited for the street to clear. When it did, he started to follow the lineup of cars ahead. Everything progressed normally, until a few seconds later when *wham,* without warning, they were jolted by a violent blow to the left side of the cab. From out of nowhere, a car had smashed against them. The sickening sound of scraping metal seemed to last an eternity as the renegade car slid along the taxi's length.

The cabbie's whistling instantly stopped, a startled obscenity taking its place as he lurched the wheel hard to the left to prevent them from being rammed onto the sidewalk. At the same time, he stomped down hard on the brake, throwing Randall forward and caused his garment bag to plummet to the floor.

As Randall groped to steady himself, he saw that a red sports car had come to a stop some yards up the street, slewed slightly across two traffic lanes.

Horns honked as the cabbie jumped from his vehicle to inspect the damage, then livid, ran to confront the other driver.

"Are you *crazy?*" he shrieked, not caring about the cars that whizzed by on the intersecting street. "Look what you've done! I can't believe it! I just can't believe it! I just *got* this cab. Lady, you'd better have insurance! *Lots* of insurance!"

The driver of the sports car remained in her seat, but her reply incensed the cabbie even more. The man started to wave his arms and shout even louder, slipping into his native Italian.

"Are you all right?" someone asked, tapping on the cab's rear window to gain Randall's attention.

He nodded and waved. He wasn't hurt, merely rattled. Why, of all times, did this have to happen now? Was the God of Transportation angry with him or something?

He righted the glasses he wore when not wearing his contacts and rescued his garment bag from the floor. Then he looked from the agitated cabbie to the empty driver's seat. He knew he had two choices: either help solve the situation or walk. And since climbing to the top of Russian Hill held no appeal at this moment— the way things were going, he'd probably trip and

tumble all the way back down to the street below and
be run over by a truck—he stepped out of the cab,
straightened his shoulders and forged ahead to the of-
fending car.

It was only as he drew nearer that he was struck by
its similarity to the car owned by his sister. Susan's car
was also a brand-new, bright red Nissan 300ZX. And
to make the coincidence even more strange, this car
bore the same dealership marking on the trunk.

Slowly, with casual curiosity, Randall's gaze
dropped to the license plate. Then he came to an
abrupt halt in the middle of the street.

He was good at details. He had been all his life. It
was an attribute that had allowed him to graduate in
the top ten percent of his law class. But he was especially good with numbers. And these numbers were
exactly the same! This *was* Susan's car!

Randall's thoughts skittered around for a reason.
Susan was in Paris. She'd been there for the past
month. Therefore, it stood to reason that her car
should be safely tucked away in the garage beneath her
apartment... not out in the street, freshly involved in
an accident, with the paint along its entire right side
deeply scratched and a portion of its right front fender
caved in!

Randall shook himself from his daze and stalked to
the open passenger window, where he leaned inside.
For a moment, he had entertained the thought that the
driver might be an irresponsible friend of Susan's, but
he had never seen this person before in his life! Small

both in height and in body type, the woman's pale
blond hair was cut extremely short and loaded with
products to make it stand out in a lion's mane of fine
spikes. Black eyeliner had been applied with a heavy
hand, as had twin slashes of dark shadow, which emphasized the hollows beneath her cheekbones. A cluster of earrings swung from her lobes, several chains of
different lengths were around her neck, and a multitude of bracelets were collected on one wrist, while a
short, black, leather miniskirt revealed an expanse of
slim, shapely thigh encased in black leggings.

"See here," he said stiffly. "Who, exactly, are you?
And why are you driving my sister's car?"

The woman—maybe he should revise that, she
looked barely out of her teens—did not pay the
slightest bit of attention to him. Her gaze remained
fixed on the street ahead, as if searching for something she had lost.

The cabbie continued to rant. "As usual! Cops are
never around when you want them!" He glared at the
girl. "You aren't going anywhere, lady, so stop acting
as if you think you are!"

Randall still reeled with shock. How had *she* gotten
possession of his sister's car? Had she stolen it? Surely
Susan didn't know her. Susan, who was extremely
protective of everything that she owned and equally
fastidious in the selection of her friends.

"Miss!" he tried again to gain her attention.

China blue eyes swiveled to meet his, instantly im-
printing their color as well as their beauty on his brain.

She turned back to the street without speaking, an intense frown on her brow. Then all at once, she stiffened.

Randall followed her gaze. A shiny black Cadillac with two dark-haired men inside had drawn to a stop on the intersecting street. There was something menacing in the way the men looked back at her. One of them laughed. Then, with a loud screech of tires, the car peeled away.

The young woman's response was immediate: she threw her, or rather, Susan's car into gear and revved the engine as if to engage in pursuit.

The cabbie screamed and jumped in her way, taking a stupid chance with his life. All the while, horns blared in the street behind them.

Randall grabbed ahold of the passenger door. "Look here!" he shouted. "You're not going to leave until you explain yourself. This is my sister's car and look what you've done to it!"

Once again china blue eyes jerked to his. Only this time, instead of remaining silent, she clipped, "If you are who you say you are, then get in. That is, if you're interested in ever seeing your sister alive again."

Randall stared at her in disbelief. Had he heard what he thought he'd heard?

"Get *in!*" she repeated fiercely.

The engine revved and the car jerked forward, enough to scare the cabbie out of the way but not enough to break Randall's hold.

Randall glanced back at the cab. *His garment bag was in there!* It was a stupid thought. Nonetheless, he clung to it for a series of seconds in the same way that a man might cling to the last bit of sanity in a world otherwise gone mad. Then he yanked the door open and dived into the familiar bucket seat.

The girl didn't hesitate. The car peeled away like a cherry red blur, taking the corner in the same direction as the black car on what had to be its two right wheel rims. It went in the same direction as the black car.

The last Randall saw of the cabbie was limited to a flash. The man was literally jumping up and down with fury.

Chapter Two

A racing engine, the squeal of tires...one foot jammed the clutch while the other stamped the accelerator. Rings flashed and bracelets jangled as one gear was shifted into another.

Randall did his best to cling to his seat. His glasses had again been knocked askew, but he couldn't take even a moment to straighten them. He wanted to shout at her to be careful, to slow down, but he didn't think that she would listen.

The Nissan slid around one corner, then another, then up and down a short hill, catching up to and then keeping close behind the black Cadillac. For a time, the two cars stayed together. Then, at a crowded intersection, the lead car shot through a red light, narrowly avoiding being hit by a delivery truck. Brakes screamed, including the Nissan's own, as Randall and the woman jerked to a stop. Other drivers on the cross street took evasive actions to avoid hitting the stalled truck. One by one, cars turned awkwardly across several lanes, packing the street in front of the Nissan.

His stomach giving what he hoped was its final lurch, Randall managed to straighten his glasses in time to see his driver jam the clutch in again and shift into first. She'd assumed a position of readiness in anticipation of a quick clearing of the street. Her short, blond hair, standing so stiffly on end, mirrored her aggressiveness, as did her tightly held lips. Randall stared at her in disbelief.

"You've got to be kidding!" he exclaimed.

Her blue eyes dismissed him as if he were a bug.

The light switched from red to green. She gunned the engine, but not one car ahead of them moved.

"Get out of the way! Get out of the *way!*" she urged, her body taut.

She leaned on the horn. Several other horns blared in accompaniment. Blandishments did no good. One car had rear-ended another, and the drivers were getting out, blocking traffic even more by their actions.

The woman threw an impatient look at the hapless Volvo nearest them and Randall could sense her desire to vaporize it. Without a doubt, if they had been sitting in one of those big pickup trucks with the huge, knobby tires that could practically climb a tree, the Volvo wouldn't have stood a chance.

Then she spotted an escape route. Ignoring the horns that now blared at them, she eased the car repeatedly back and forth until at last, they were able to slip from the far lane of traffic onto the curb, then past a crowd of gawkers and a lamppost, to fall with a resounding thump into the intersecting street.

The way ahead of them was clear, and Randall again braced himself. A succession of corners were taken at a fast clip, and almost miraculously, a few seconds later, they were farther up their original street, the snarl of traffic fast disappearing behind them. A police car approached from the opposite direction.

Randall glanced at his companion, wondering what her response to the patrol car would be. Would it make her slow down? Give up the chase? But she paid it about as much attention as she paid him. She was intent on only one thing, the resumption of her search for the black Cadillac.

He decided to try to attract the attention of the police himself by yelling "Hey!" and waving his arms, but they, too, seemed to be concentrating on other matters, most likely the choked intersection.

Randall settled back in his seat and threw the woman a look of disgruntlement, only to see that she had stiffened. Then he saw why. She had spotted the other car. It was pulled up next to an alleyway with the two men standing outside. One was tall and thin, the other short and built like a stump. Both were looking with disgust at a flattened tire.

Quickly adjusting the Nissan's direction, she swerved close by. "Hey! You guys!" she yelled, slowing almost to a stop. "Do you need some help?"

Two heads jerked up. When the men recognized her, both of them stiffened. Laughing at their predicament, she taunted, "I'll call AAA…in about a week! Next time, think twice before you try to follow me. I *don't* like it!'' That said, the red car shot away, her laughter continuing to float on the breeze.

Randall shifted position. He wondered what would happen next. He soon found out. She turned into a parking garage and after tucking the car safely into an out-of-the-way space, twisted around to look at him.

"So," she said, "you're Susan's brother." She didn't sound the least impressed.

Randall hadn't expected timidity from her and he didn't get it. She was still very much the aggressor in this affair, intent upon keeping him firmly in his place. Randall decided to pull himself up a rung or two.

"Just what the hell did you mean by telling me my sister is in some sort of danger? Do you even *know* my sister?"

Her response was quick. "Of course, I know her! How do you think I have use of her car? Do you think I stole it?"

Now it was Randall's turn to laugh. "Lady, I wouldn't put anything past you." He watched, satisfied, as her slender fingers tightened on the steering wheel. "Anyway," he continued. "My sister's in Paris. She's been there for a month and isn't scheduled to return until the end of next month. She's spending the summer with a friend."

"She came back early."

"Why?"

The woman's blue eyes narrowed. "If I mentioned the name Michael James, would it mean anything to you?"

"Should it?"

She gave a brittle smile. "I'd think so. Since Susan and Michael are to be married."

Randall jerked forward in his seat. "No! Now I know we're talking about two different people. My sister is a college senior. She's majoring in Business and plans to run the world in a couple of years. She's certainly not going to marry anyone, at least, not for a long, long time!"

"She's marrying my brother in six weeks. At least, that was the original plan."

Randall stared at her, his clean-cut, boyishly handsome features incredulous. What she said was impossible. Susan wouldn't do something like that! "I don't believe you. You're making this up."

"I wish I were."

He began to bluster, still not believing her. "I demand some kind of proof! I'm not going to just sit here and listen while you—"

"Demand all you want," she said, interrupting. "It won't do any good. The only person who can confirm what I'm saying is Susan, and she's in hiding, along with my brother."

"Why? Why is she hiding?" Impulsively he looked back toward the street. "Do those two men have something to do with this?"

A thin smile touched her lips at his belated realization. "Do I have your attention now?"

"What's going on here?" Randall demanded, suddenly deadly serious. He had been knocked off balance. First, by the accident, then by the wildness of the chase. But this lack of centeredness would not continue. "Who *are* you? Why are you telling me this? Surely if it's true, you've gone to the police. You *have* gone to the police, haven't you?"

She ignored his string of questions to ask a question of her own. "You're a lawyer, aren't you? I seem to remember Susan saying that you were . . . the one time she mentioned you."

"The *one* time she mentioned me?" Randall felt a quick stab of hurt. He and Susan were close; at least, he had always thought so. That she could be so deeply involved with someone and neglect to tell him! Then to hear that she had barely spoken of him! The idea unnerved him, and that reaction was exactly what the woman seated next to him seemed to want! He recognized this when he caught the look of satisfaction that ran deeply in her eyes as he recoiled from his thoughts. She *wanted* to keep him off balance. Make him doubt himself. Make him wonder about Susan. And she was doing a darned good job!

"What if I am a lawyer?" he retorted grimly, going back to her previous question.

"Then you can be useful," she replied.

"Doing what?"

"Helping my brother."

Randall lost the final curb on his patience. "Look, lady! You have some kind of nerve, do you know that? What's your brother done, anyway? And why would Susan—?"

A car wheeled into the garage, making both of them start. It turned out to be a bedraggled old Plymouth, not the sleek black Cadillac that they had both imagined. But it was enough to spur the woman into action. Once again, without allowing Randall time to protest, she started the car and lurched out of the parking space.

This time, though, Randall was determined not to be such a compliant captive. His hand snaked out to entrap hers, holding it on the gear-shift knob as she started to shift into first. The car's engine strained, impatient to be away.

China blue eyes flashed angrily into his. "Let go," she warned. "Or I won't be responsible for what happens."

"I'm a hell of a lot bigger than you are...or haven't you noticed?"

His soft response made her lip curl. "How typical of certain segments of the male population. Always thinking in terms of the physical. I was referring to your sister and my brother. If we don't do something to help *them,* and *quickly,* it will be too late."

"What if I still don't believe you?" he challenged. His hand stayed where it was, keeping her immobile.

She didn't cringe from the intensity of his gaze, meeting it, instead, with an equal intensity of her own. "Are you willing to take that kind of chance?"

Drawing upon his years of experience in the practice of law, Randall took a moment to study her. His conclusion: if she was lying, she believed every word.

His fingers slowly loosened.

Without delay, she set the car in motion, firming her jaw as they slipped onto the city streets.

Once again, Randall braced himself for the unknown.

FRANCESCA JAMES ADJUSTED her grip on the steering wheel and expertly skimmed along with the traffic. Instinctively she headed toward the tiny room she had rented on a weekly basis in one of the seedier sections of the city. At the moment, all she wanted was to close her eyes for a few seconds of uninterrupted peace and dream of the way things used to be. But it didn't seem as if life was going to return to normal anytime soon. Especially not since she had lumbered herself with an unwilling guest. The coincidence had been staggering. She had sideswiped a taxi, and that taxi had been carrying Susan's brother, *the lawyer*. It was almost like a gift from heaven, one she couldn't refuse.

Her gaze slid over the tall, leanly muscled man at her side. In all likelihood, he thought her totally insane. And possibly she was, for losing her temper like that. Hopefully she hadn't made things worse by chasing those men and taunting them. But the strain of the past two weeks had finally caused her to snap. She had stepped out of the club and had seen them sitting in their car, grinning at her so smugly, as if to rub in the fact that all they had to do was wait. They seemed to think that once she had located her brother, it would be a simple thing for them to follow her. She had acted from instinct, not intellect.

A shiver ran up Francesca's spine. She had to find Michael! She had to be sure that he was safe and that he would continue to be safe! But had her crazy chase accomplished anything? She slid her companion another glance. He was pale and his fingers were curled tightly into the seat cushion, as if he feared for his life. Not exactly reassuring. But she needed his brain, not his brawn.

Certainly no other lawyer she'd talked to had wanted to help. The case wasn't strong enough; nor was enough money involved. And when she mentioned the name of the group that Michael was in trouble with, those who knew it by reputation had acted as if she'd had the plague and could somehow infect them over the telephone line. They couldn't disconnect fast enough.

Her only hope now seemed to be the strength of a blood relationship. With this man, Susan was the key. Her ace in the hole. And she had to play it for all that it was worth. Not that she didn't care about Susan's well-being. She did! Susan was one of the nicest girls Michael had ever dated. Francesca very much approved of gaining Susan for a sister-in-law. However, it was Michael she was most concerned about at present, because it was Michael who would pay the highest price if nothing was done. Susan could walk away; Michael couldn't.

In the beginning, Francesca had received only one brief warning of what her brother planned to do. Her second notice came when he called to inform her that it was done. He was supposed to call again, to get the name of the lawyer she had hired to come to his assistance, but the call never came. A week passed, then nearly another. Uncertainty had almost driven her insane! She had tried to work, but couldn't concentrate.

All her life, she had watched out for Michael, who was two years her junior. She'd been the emotionally steadier of the two. Michael was the sensitive dreamer. She was the one grounded in reality. Only this time, it was a reality she couldn't deal with. Not by herself. She needed help. And if she didn't get it . . .

A haze of tears rushed into her eyes, tears that she savagely blinked away. She didn't have time for weakness. Not now! She had to be strong! She had to be fearless!

"Where are we going?" the man at her side asked after a period of silence.

Francesca attempted to swallow the lump of emotion that had settled in her throat. She wasn't totally successful. As a result, her reply sounded gruff. "You'll find out soon enough."

His gaze swept over her in disfavor. "There's no need to be rude. I'm here, aren't I? I'm prepared to listen to what you have to say."

"How magnanimous of you."

His mouth tightened. "Make up your mind. Either you want my help or you don't! But don't waste my time. I'm not in the mood to play games."

"Neither am I."

"At least we agree on something!"

Francesca blinked back another onslaught of tears. She didn't *want* to be doing this; she didn't *want* Michael to be in such terrible trouble.

She drew the car into a makeshift parking spot that was shielded from the street by a partially tumbled down wall and slipped easily from the driver's seat.

"Follow me," she directed, sparing her companion only a brief glance before starting to walk away.

"We can talk right here," he declared, refusing to budge, drawing her back around.

Francesca glanced at him coolly. "You can. But you'll be by yourself."

He jabbed his dark-rimmed glasses more firmly into place. "I'm not following you if I don't know where we're going."

She allowed a small, mocking smile. "Why not? Are you afraid for your virtue?"

The muscles of his jaw tightened.

"I promise I won't try to ravish you," she continued, heaping derision on top of derision. "You're perfectly safe with me."

The car door jerked open and he piled out, mumbling something beneath his breath.

"I'm sorry, what did you say?" she asked, just to goad him.

A stormy frown darkened his brow. "I said that this better not be someone's idea of a joke!"

Francesca only wished that it was. She could be leading him to a room where his friends would be waiting. They would sing Happy Birthday, or whatever, to celebrate the occasion, then they would be off again in a couple of hours, all having had a wonderful time. "It's no joke," she answered stiffly.

This time when she turned away, he followed.

Randall kept close watch on the ramrod straight back as it moved through the accumulating gloom. Streetlights were few and far between in this area of the city, even as the feeling of being watched became stronger. Shadows seemed deeper, alleyways less inviting. The gazes of the people they passed on the sidewalks slid over them quickly in silent estimation before sliding just as quickly away again. And when someone's eyes did linger, it wasn't from friendliness.

The evening had a distinct chill both in atmosphere and in temperature. His days in the mugginess of Chicago had thinned his blood. He wished that he had his coat, but it was still in the cab, in his garment bag.

Hopefully the cabbie would drop the bag off at his apartment and he wouldn't have to spend the rest of that night or all day tomorrow trying to locate his possessions at the cab company's office. If he managed to make it through this night, that was.

Randall's thoughts were drawn back to the woman walking slightly ahead of him, and he couldn't prevent a purely masculine reaction. She was very different from the type of woman he normally associated with, her choice of dress, makeup and accessories more than a little unusual and her personality abrasive. But she certainly did look good in that snug-fitting mini! All slim and trim with a tiny waist, nice derriere, sleek graceful legs, and in a package that could be little more than five feet tall. The rest of her was covered by a lightweight leather jacket, a long netlike scarf that she wore around her neck, not her hair, and a pair of soft black, ankle boots.

Who was she? *What* was she? Was she telling the truth? Or was this some kind of confidence game that he had stumbled upon? Snare an unwary tourist, bring him to an unknown destination, render him unconscious and then rob him.

The only stopper to this line of reasoning was Susan's car. Because it *was* Susan's car.

The woman paused at a narrow doorway that led into a rundown building and pushed her way inside. A long row of stairs rose directly to the second floor from the tiny hall. The area smelled faintly of unwashed bodies, old food and mustiness.

China blue eyes waited for his reaction.

Randall swallowed his disgust and met her look head-on, not allowing his gaze to waver.

She led the way upstairs and paused at a door immediately off the second landing. "This is it," she said, motioning for him to enter.

Randall hesitated only a second before stepping inside. He tensed for whatever might be waiting, for whoever might be waiting. He would fight if he had to! But there was no one to battle. When she flicked on a small, ratty lamp that sat on one corner of a chipped chest of drawers, the tiny room was shown to be empty of accomplices. A sagging bed held the place of honor as the room's major occupant, its threadbare spread having seen better days. But at least the atmosphere had improved here. A plastic tube of air freshener was open full blast, and a window had been left up to allow the chilly breeze to waft in.

Randall said nothing as he turned to look at her.

She shrugged out of her jacket, tossing it carelessly onto the bed. The scarf fell on top of it. "I'd offer you a drink, but I'm fresh out."

"I don't want anything," Randall replied.

She went to pull the window down, but settled for leaving it slightly ajar. The room was better off cool than airless. "Not even water, I'm afraid," she persisted.

Randall stood in his day-worn suit, in the new shoes his feet had become tired of wearing, in the tie that he had loosened in the cab, and he just wanted her to get to the point. "Why don't you try telling me what's going on?" he said.

With one part of his mind, Randall registered that the rest of her body was as perfect as everything else. She had a slender neck and slim shoulders, and her breasts were perfectly formed. She frowned when she became aware of his estimating look and he quickly pulled his gaze away.

She motioned for him to sit in the only available chair. It was faded and worn, but appeared fairly clean. Randall shook his head.

"Have you ever heard of the Massey brothers?" she asked, also choosing to remain standing. "Philip and Ted? They're from Los Angeles."

"I'm afraid not," he replied. She sighed, and he wondered if she did so out of relief.

"Well, they're in the music business. They own a fairly large record label that a number of well-known artists work with." She named a few people and groups, some of whom Randall recognized.

"What does that have to do with your brother?" he asked.

"He's a singer-song writer."

"And . . . ?" he prompted.

"My brother did something that made the Massey brothers angry."

"What did he do?"

"He took possession of the master tape to his latest album."

"By *took,* do you mean he stole it?"

"It was his!" she said, instantly defensive.

Randall shook his head. "Lady, you've made a big mistake. I can't help you. I'm the wrong kind of lawyer. I specialize in civil law for corporations, not in criminal defense."

"But I've tried everyone else!"

"Surely not."

"No one will even *listen!*"

Randall shrugged. "Then my advice is to keep trying. There are lots of lawyers around. Surely you've missed one or two. Now, this has been an extremely long day for me. I've been on the move since five o'clock this morning. I'm tired. I want to go home, go to bed and sleep for at least the next twelve hours. Are you going to take me home, or do I have to hunt down another cab?"

"What about Susan?" the woman asked.

"Susan's a big girl. She can take care of herself. Unless she was a participant in the theft, she's on pretty safe ground." He walked to the door, wanting nothing more than to be gone from this place.

"And what if she was?" the woman challenged.

The provocation worked. Randall slowly turned around. "You'd better be careful what you say," he warned.

Her chin lifted, her attitude defiant. "It's all right for you to call my brother a thief, but it's not all right for me to say the same thing about your sister. Is that the way it is?"

"You're the one who claims your brother is in trouble for stealing his—whatever it is."

"His tape! But it's his! It's *his* property. He wrote every song himself and even produced it."

"Then why is he in trouble?"

Her gaze faltered, but quickly returned with renewed spirit. "It's the Massey brothers who are the thieves! Just when my brother's career is about to take off, they want to destroy him. If you knew anything about the music industry, you'd know that the Massey brothers are bad news. People just don't cross them!''

"Your brother did," Randall said softly. "And if he's anything like you, I don't blame the Massey brothers for being angry."

He pulled the door open. He didn't care if he had to walk home. Miles and hills didn't seem to matter anymore.

She called urgently, "You're not much of a brother if you're willing to stand by and do nothing while your sister's in danger of being hurt!"

Perhaps it was this terrible day, a day that didn't seem to want to end, a nightmare of Homeric proportions. But something caused Randall to snap. There was no way he was going to let someone who knew absolutely nothing about his familial relationships make such a judgment against him.

With exaggerated calm, he closed the door and retraced his steps until he stood directly across from her. He considered the fact that the top of her head came barely past the middle of his chest, the fact that, for a second, he thought he saw the sheen of tears in her eyes, the fact that, for all her outlandish clothing and overdone makeup, she was arrestingly attractive and that her body was singularly the nicest he had seen in a very long time. But none of that seemed to matter.

With deliberate intent, he reached out and clasped her shoulders and gave her a tiny shake. "You know nothing about the way I feel. Nothing! If Susan needed me, really needed me, there isn't anything I wouldn't do for her. I don't expect you to understand that. Few people do in this day and age. But that's the way it is for us. I love Susan, and she loves me!"

The young woman stiffened. She would not back down. "You don't think much of yourself, do you?" she accused. "You think you're the only person in the world who loves a brother or sister like that. What arrogance! What self-centeredness! A *lot* of other people feel the same way. Not just you! I'd do anything for my brother. Anything! And I've *proved* it! Have you?"

Chapter Three

The pretty face remained defiant. In spite of himself and in spite of the situation, Randall found himself wanting to kiss her. The urge was one of the most overwhelming, out-of-the-blue lightning strikes of emotion that he had ever experienced. She was challenging him, calling him names, and all he wanted was to press his lips to hers, feel her lips part, feel her body grow warm and yielding...and feel her start to respond.

Randall drew back, shocked. He had been instantly attracted to certain women before. He'd even had one or two deeply satisfying relationships as a result. But never had it been anything like this. And with someone like her. What was the matter with him? He cleared his throat, trying to salvage what he could of the situation. "I, ah—I didn't mean to insult you. I understand that other people might feel the same way, but I—" He broke off, deciding to start again with more sincerity. "I care for Susan just as much as you obviously care for your brother."

"So you'll help?"

She was daring him to refuse.

"I still think you'd be better off finding someone who knows the field. I don't. I'd probably be more of a detriment than a help."

"Having you is better than having no one," she replied.

He looked at her curiously. "What is it about the Massey brothers that frightens everyone so much?"

"They don't mind hurting people if they don't get their way."

"Then this really is a matter for the police. Why haven't you called them?"

She spun away to the window and stayed there, looking out.

Randall's normally cautious nature warred with his recurring feelings of attraction. Slowly he asked, "Is it because your brother actually did steal the tape? And you're afraid that if you call the police, he'll be in trouble with them, too?"

"The tape was *his*," she said stubbornly. "It was his creation!"

"You can't expect me to help if you're not willing to tell the truth. *All* of it."

She turned to look at him, uncertainty clouding her eyes. Then she asked quietly, "What do you want to know?"

"Everything," he said.

WHEN IT CAME DOWN TO IT, Francesca didn't know if she should trust him or not. She desperately needed his help. He *was* a lawyer. But what if after hearing everything, he still insisted upon calling the police? What if he only made things worse for Michael instead of better?

She took a deep breath after making a decision. "You may not recognize Michael's name now, but one day you will. Everyone will. He's good. Very good. That's why the Masseys tried to steal him away from Glass House Records last fall. They saw his potential and wanted him to work for them. But Michael refused. The people at Glass House were and still are his friends. They had faith in him when no one else did. And when it seemed that things were finally going to start to happen for him, he didn't want to turn his back on them. He'd seen people do that kind of thing before and he didn't like it.

"Of course, the Masseys didn't like being turned down. Especially Philip Massey. He got nasty, and Michael ended up throwing a drink in his face right in the middle of one of those 'power restaurants' in Los Angeles, the kind where everyone who's anyone goes to make a deal. Then Michael walked out. Later, he heard from someone that Philip Massey was livid because he'd been treated like that in front of everyone.

"Michael shouldn't have done it. He'd heard the rumors about the Masseys. That was another reason why he didn't want to work for them, but he said he just couldn't help himself. The man was so obnoxious.

"Things went along fine for a time. Michael thought the whole thing had died down. Then about three months ago, a rumor started that the Masseys were going to buy Glass House. The label was always on the shaky side financially, but suddenly, things got worse. Then the rumors came true.

"Philip Massey called Michael. He told him that *he* was the person behind the takeover and that he was going to bury him—that he could kiss his career goodbye. It was as if getting back at Michael had become some kind of personal vendetta with him. His ego just couldn't take the public humiliation."

"Precisely what is this tape that your brother took?"

"Like I said before, it's the master of his latest album. All the tracks had been laid and the tape was just waiting for final approval before it went out to be made into compact discs and cassettes. It's taken Michael months to get to this point. Years, really. And he's tremendously excited about it now. He thinks it's his best work. So does everyone who's heard it. It should be his breakthrough album. It will transform him from being a performer for a small alternative audience to being a performer for the world!"

"If he's not buried," Randall surmised.

Her nod was jerky.

He thought for a moment. "How can the Masseys destroy his career?"

"By disrupting the distribution of his album, delaying the release of his singles, interfering with his appearance schedule, making a mess of his videos or refusing to pay for any videos at all. Even more importantly, they could refuse the material he already has on the tape. They could tell him that some or all of it is inferior and make him keep redoing it. For no real reason, just for spite."

"You seem to know quite a lot about it. Are you in the record business, too?"

"No."

Francesca refused to say more. *She* wasn't the person this was about. Michael was. And she had already told Randall Peters all that he needed to know. Depending on others was something that went against the grain of her normal inclinations. She liked to handle all her problems on her own, to rely only on herself. It was much safer that way.

"And the tape belongs to him," he said, testing her information.

She hesitated then admitted, "As the artist, Michael owns a certain percentage. It's in his contract."

"Then why—"

"Possession is what counts here! He's afraid Philip Massey will destroy it!"

Randall Peters paced to the opposite side of the room and came back again, a frustrated frown marking his brow. "How did Susan get involved in all of this? She never said a word to me. Not a word!"

He was still fighting against believing that his sister could do such a thing, but Francesca could see that he was starting to lose ground, starting to doubt his earlier convictions. She felt a light burst of sympathy for him, but hardened herself against it. She shrugged. "She met Michael through a mutual friend. They fell in love. What more can I say?"

"You can stop being so darned obstinate for one thing," he snapped, his frustration spilling out. "How did she get involved in this mess?"

"I don't know!" Francesca cried. She was perfectly aware that he had just referred to his sister's involvement with Michael as a "mess," but there was little she could do about it at the moment. "All I know is that she's with him. Someone told me they'd seen her."

"Someone?"

"A friend."

"How did you get the use of her car? Did this *friend* give you that, too?"

His mind seemed fixated on the car. "You still think I stole it, don't you?" she complained.

"Like brother, like sister. It wouldn't be the first time larceny ran in a family."

Francesca objected to the slight against her family name without thinking. Her hand whipped out, making contact with his cheek even before she knew it had moved. His head jerked, the imprint of her fingers showing white on his skin.

Within a second, he had whipped off his glasses and was glaring at her.

Francesca did her best to brave out his anger. She couldn't afford to back down. Not now. Not when she was so close to achieving her goal.

She gazed defiantly into those pale gray eyes and unwillingly registered the fact that Susan's brother was an extremely nice looking man. He had even features set in a pleasing face, good bone structure, a straight nose that was neither too big nor too narrow, a mouth that looked as if it curved often into a smile, and a strong jaw. Tall and athletic, with light brown hair and good taste in clothes, he was the epitome of the boy next door that mothers loved and fathers trusted, and that available women of any age found extraordinarily appealing.

Francesca jerked her attention back to the situation, not letting herself dwell on anything so distracting as his looks. Her answer was sarcastic. "I wish I had a note telling you that it's all right for me to use Susan's car. But I forgot to ask for one. I never really expected to have to use it. She loaned the car to me the day before she left for Europe. I'd been having trouble with my car, and since it was going to cost a mint to repair it—more than it was worth, actually—she thought the perfect solution was for me to drive hers while she was away. That would keep it from sitting unused in her garage for most of the summer. I didn't want to do it, but she insisted. Now I wish I'd listened to my first instinct!"

"So will she when she sees what you've done to it."

"I'll pay to have it repaired!"

His glance went disparagingly around the shabby room. "With what?" he asked.

Francesca drew a quick breath. If this had been the best she could do for herself, his derogatory dismissal would have been wounding. It was so easy for people to judge when they judged from a safe distance. When they didn't know the struggles to survive that went on in another person's everyday life.

He must have been thinking along the same lines because a flash of regret passed through his pale eyes. In a delaying move, he set his glasses back into place before apologizing. "I'm sorry. I didn't mean to insult you."

"You keep saying that!" she retorted. "But you keep insulting me. I'm not asking for charity. I'm willing to pay your fee. Just name it! Tell me what it is! I have two thousand dollars saved. I can probably scrape together more."

"I don't want your money!"

"Then what is it that you *do* want?"

Randall wasn't sure anymore. This morning, his wants had been simple. He'd wanted his plane to take off on time from O'Hare, then later, he'd wanted to have himself, his plane and his luggage all touch down somewhere near the same intersecting meridian and parallel, preferably in California. San Francisco to be exact. Next, he had wanted nothing more than his own apartment and his own bed. Now, everything seemed to have shifted totally beyond his control. If Susan truly were in trouble... "I have to be sure you're telling the truth," he said.

Francesca threw up her hands, vexed. "I don't *have* proof! All I have is my word, and that doesn't seem to be good enough!" She paused, thinking. "Call your sister. Call her in Paris! If she's not there, then maybe you'll believe me."

"I talked to her earlier this week. Everything was fine. She didn't give me any sense that she was worried about anything."

"Situations change. Call her. What's the matter? Are you afraid? Do the Massey brothers frighten you, too?"

Randall ignored her attempt at bullying. "Do you have a phone?"

"There's one downstairs, if it works."

"Why don't we see?"

He motioned for her to proceed to the door. She eyed him suspiciously, then lifted her chin and walked ahead of him into the hall.

The pay phone was to one side of the lobby, surrounded by an ever-expanding wall of graffiti. There were names, phone numbers and comments. Some were funny, some risqué and some merely crude. There were also numerous drawings along those same lines.

Randall lifted the receiver, dropped in the proper coinage and waited for a dial tone. Then turning slightly so that the woman couldn't see what he was doing, he punched in the appropriate numbers of both his private long-distance telephone charge card and the villa where Susan was a guest. He was barely conscious of the fact that his mind filed away numbers with an ease that most people found dismaying. A series of clicks later, a telephone on the other side of the world rang.

"Susan Peters, *s'il vous plaît,*" he requested as soon as the call was answered.

A voice responded rapidly in French.

Randall's knowledge of the language was limited to two years in high school, and that was a very long time ago. He tried again in English. "Susan Peters? I wish to speak with Susan Peters? I'm sorry. I don't speak French well enough to—"

He stopped when he was interrupted by heavily accented English. "Mademoiselle es not 'ere. She 'as returned to 'er 'ome. If you wish to speak with Madame Chiasson, she will return soon. I will 'ave 'er call you."

Randall didn't answer right away. Susan had returned to San Francisco, just as the woman standing next to him had said. He turned to look at her. His eyes narrowed. She met his look with level certainty.

"*Monsieur?*" the voice from across a continent and an ocean prompted.

Susan had returned home, but she hadn't called him. Once again, the idea hurt. She hadn't told him about her return. She hadn't told him about her relationship with Michael James—if it could be completely believed. Then Randall's mind leapt to the fact

that he'd been away for five days. If she had tried to
contact him, he wouldn't know about it yet! Not until
he collected the messages from his answering machine.

The thought immediately lightened his heavy frown,
which caused the woman watching him to lift her own
finely arched brows in inquiry.

Randall excused himself from the servant at the
villa. He disconnected for only a second before add-
ing more coins and jabbing in another, shorter series
of numbers. Once he reached his answering machine,
he contributed even more numbers. Then he listened
as one message reeled off after another.

The woman's eyes were fixed on his face. They were
a color he wondered if he'd ever be able to forget.

Then came the message he had been waiting for.
Susan's voice was hurried and tense. "Randall . . . it's
me, Susan. I can't explain now. Not in just a minute
or two. But I'm back in San Francisco. A friend of
mine is in trouble. If you get home in time, call me at
this number." She recited a number Randall didn't
recognize. "If not—" She said something to someone in the room with her, the words muffled, rushed.
When she uncovered the mouthpiece again, her voice
was underscored with urgency. "Randall . . . please,
don't worry. I'm okay. I'll—I'll call you again as soon
as I can."

Randall's grip tightened as he listened to the end of
the machine's taped messages. There were no addi-
tional calls from Susan. Normally so calm, she, like

him, enjoyed having a solid idea of where she was going and what she was going to do when she got there. It was upsetting to hear her sound so fearful!

He jammed the receiver back on the hook before hurriedly entering the number that she had left for him.

"What is it? What's happening?" the woman at his elbow demanded.

"Wait," Randall ordered.

A man answered on the second ring. Randall's stomach tensed. "Susan Peters, please. This is her brother."

"She ain't here," the man said, giving the impression that he was about to hang up.

"She left a message for me to call this number!" Randall said hurriedly to stop him.

"Hey, I can't help that. She still ain't here."

"Is it all right with you if I leave a message?" Randall's patience was wearing thin. Fear clawed at him as he finally began to admit that this situation was real.

"Sure, if you want to," the man said. "But I doubt she'll be back. She just crashed here for a couple of days, then she left."

"Is this some kind of hotel?" Randall demanded.

The man's laugh was short and disagreeable. "My wife seems to think it is."

"If Susan comes by or if she calls, tell her that I'm back in town and to get in touch with me as quickly as she can. She knows the number. Do you have that?"

"Sure, I have it. Call her brother. Anything else?"

Randall didn't know whether the man was being intentionally obtuse or if he was just plain stupid.

"No. That's all," he said. "Just tell her to call."

"Right. Will do."

Randall sagged against the wall after he hung up. "I doubt that will do much good."

"So now you believe me." The woman standing next to him gave Randall no quarter in the face of his enlightenment.

He shifted away from the wall. "Yes, I believe you," he said quietly. He was both bone weary and afraid.

"And you're willing to help?" she persisted.

"Yes, I'm willing to help," he agreed.

She released a short breath, as if some inborn tension had been lifted. "All right. At least that's settled. Now, what we have to do is plan our next move."

She turned to go back upstairs.

"Here?" Randall asked. He did not move.

She swung round to face him. "Can you think of a better place?"

"My apartment?"

"If we know that Susan is with Michael, what makes you think the Masseys don't know it, too?"

Randall frowned. "I don't see where that makes any difference."

"Someone will be watching your place. Just as they were watching mine. I don't think they know about this one yet."

"But if she calls—"

"She'll leave another message. But don't expect her to tell you where she is. Your phone could be tapped. And she'll know that."

"Oh, surely not."

A slow, mocking smile pulled at her lips. "You've entered another world, Mr. Peters. One where people don't play by a particular set of rules. Particularly men like Philip Massey." Her gaze dropped to Randall's clothing. "Tomorrow, we'll find you something different to wear."

Randall, too, looked down at his custom-made suit. "There's absolutely nothing wrong with the way I'm dressed!"

"Not in the financial district, no. But where we're going, you'll stick out like a sore thumb."

She started up the stairs again.

Randall watched her in silence, momentarily mesmerized by the rhythmic sway of her compact hips. His first instinct was to follow her, to concern himself with nothing but the intriguing possibilities that might evolve from their continued association. But he resisted this baser motive when he realized that it was corrupt. If he went with her, it had to be for one reason and one reason only: to help rescue his sister from a situation she could not possibly have fully foreseen.

To keep his mind on this higher purpose as he climbed the stairs, he challenged grumpily, "If you want to talk about sore thumbs, what about Susan's car? It's not exactly a shy and retiring color that blends in with the scenery. It's as bright a red as it's humanly possible to mix. You couldn't sneak up on anyone if you tried."

"Beggars can't be choosers, Mr. Peters. It's all I have."

"My car is white," he offered.

"How much horse power does it have?"

"I try to be a responsible citizen of the Earth, Miss—Mrs.—Ms.—I'll be damned if I know your name!"

"Call me Frankie," she said.

She didn't look like a Frankie. "Short for what?" he asked.

She didn't answer.

When they arrived at her door, she opened it with expert ease even though the hardware was about to fall off.

"My car," he said, "would be adequate for our purpose. It's not exotic, but it definitely would blend in."

For the first time in their acquaintance, real amusement lighted her eyes. "Has it ever been over forty miles an hour in its life?"

"Yes, of course!" he said defensively. Once again, he felt as if his manhood was being questioned.

"I'll keep it in mind."

His answering glance was sour, which only made her smile grow stronger, revealing even, white teeth and a dimple in her left cheek, which left Randall with the certain knowledge that no matter how hard he tried to fight it, that dimple was going to drive him absolutely wild!

Chapter Four

Randall's gaze moved from the bed to the chair. One didn't look any more inviting than the other. "This is ridiculous," he complained, standing stiffly just inside the door. "We could go somewhere else."

"Don't worry," she assured him. "It doesn't have too many bugs." As proof, she sat down on the bedcover.

Randall included the rest of the room in his jaundiced view. The wallpaper was faded and peeling in spots, a cheap print was hanging cockeyed on its mount, the spotted carpet concealed God knew what. "I don't like this place," he concluded.

"It begins to grow on you. Give it a few days."

"I'll give it fifteen minutes."

At that moment, a fight broke out in the room next door. Raised voices and the sounds of bodies crashing into furniture came through the paper-thin walls. "It even has entertainment!" she quipped. The fight subsided almost as quickly as it had begun. Still Randall would not be prodded into a better humor.

"Fifteen minutes," he repeated.

She leaned back on her outspread hands. "Then what are you going to do?"

"What I've been trying to do all day—go home."

She shook her head. "I've already told you. They're watching your home."

"Let them."

"I thought you were going to help."

"I am! We can get together tomorrow after I—"

"We're together now."

Randall stared at her. "Look, Miss—Frankie. I don't see that it makes any difference if I go to my apartment. They don't know me. They won't know who I am."

"They will after you've shown them."

Randall paced across the floor. "There has to be a way."

"There is. You stay here, with me."

"No."

"I'll even give you the bed. It sags a little on one side, but if you stay close to the opposite edge, you'll be all right."

"No!"

"Why not?" she shot back. "I've already assured you that I'm not lusting after your body."

Randall wondered if he wouldn't have been better off still trapped in the Phoenix airport! In exasperation, he said, "I'm not going to stay here. Period."

"Where are we going, then?"

We! he thought with distaste.

"We are almost family," she continued. "When my brother marries your sister—"

"It will be a cold day in hell!" he completed.

She smiled, seeming to enjoy his displeasure. Randall's glare didn't faze her.

He stuffed his hands into the pockets of his slacks. His clothes were beginning to feel like a second skin, as if soon, he wouldn't be able to even pry them off. "I have an idea," he said after a minute.

"What?"

"I know a place where we can stay. And along the way, we can pick up my car."

"I like Susan's car."

"I'm sure you do."

"I also feel safe here."

"How can you? Look around."

"No one's bothered me—"

"Yet!" he insisted.

To lend credence to his words, the fight next door broke out again. This time, the voices were louder, the tumbling more fierce. A body was thrown against the wall nearest the bed and a fist burst through the thin wallboard.

Frankie looked at the detached forearm, then at the gaping hole left when the arm was withdrawn. After a moment, she stood up. "This place where we're going, does it have cable?"

Randall marveled at her audacity. "Yes. I'm sure it does. Why?"

"Because I don't like to be bored."

Without a backward glance, she walked to the door, her back straight, her demeanor unbeaten, as if it had been her idea all the time to leave this place, not his. He was only along for the ride.

A small smile tugged at Randall's lips as once again, he followed her.

"TURN IN AT THE NEXT entrance," Randall directed when they neared the building where he worked. Whenever he was away from the city for more than a day, he left his car in his contract parking space in the garage next door to his office. He felt it received better care there than at the airport garage. Frankie followed his instructions with expert skill. "Go two aisles then take a right." Soon, the blunt lines of his white six-year-old Honda Civic hatchback came into view. "Right here," he said.

The Nissan stopped and as his companion noted the Corvette and the Ferrari that were parked on either side of Randall's car, she silently shook her head in mock reproach.

He ignored her disdain. "I'll back my car out and you can put this one in its place." He reached to unlatch the door.

"Don't forget. You promised," she reminded.

Did she expect him to bolt for freedom the instant he was out of her clutches?

"I said I'd help," Randall answered, looking directly into her eyes. "I'm not the type of person to go back on my word."

He could see that she didn't fully believe him, but she made no further protest. As he got out of the red sports car and approached his own, more sensible mode of transportation, he felt her eyes bore into him. He fumbled with the keys before finally managing to unlock the door. Then he slid inside, started the engine and reversed out of the slot.

While Randall waited for her to catch up, he had the oddest sensation that none of this was real. For all he knew, he was still thirty thousand feet in the air, speeding over some vast western desert, and when he woke, he would discover that—

She plopped into the seat next to him, her bracelets jangling a defiant tune. "You can drive this time," she allowed, "but after this, you'd better let me. I doubt you've had much experience in evasive tactics."

He wasn't dreaming. It was real. He stared at her. "And you have?" he asked.

"Enough," she claimed.

"Yet you still hit my cab."

"Wasn't that lucky?" she asked brightly.

"For whom?" he grouched.

She turned to settle a small suitcase onto the back seat. "Quit complaining and drive."

Randall shook his head. "Aren't you just the least bit concerned that I might be dangerous? You don't know me from Adam, yet you're getting ready to spend the night with me. Aren't you worried that I might be some sort of a crazed maniac?"

The dimple appeared in her left cheek. "Susan said you were nicely respectable, if a little stuffy on occasion."

"The *one* time she mentioned me?" The remark still rankled, even if it had only been used to get to him. Still, Susan had shown that she could do other things to surprise him. Might there be a grain of truth to this? What if she had only mentioned him once?

Frankie nodded.

Randall rammed the car into gear and to completely humiliate him, it balked. Not only was it not in the same league engine-wise with his sister's high-powered sports car, it also needed a tune-up.

To his relief, they proceeded smoothly when the engine warmed, and Randall directed their path toward the Marina District.

If Paul only knew what he was about to do, they might not remain best friends for long. Making use of his house while he and Allison were away on a belated honeymoon was not the same thing as looking after it, as he'd been asked. But he doubted that Paul would give even a passing thought to what he, Randall, was doing. Not as besotted as Paul was with his wife of several months. And not that Randall blamed him. Allison was special. The two of them had been through such an ordeal before finally getting together.

Speaking of ordeals...Randall glanced at the woman seated next to him. He didn't know what to make of her. She acted so tough sometimes. Was she really that tough? Or was her show of toughness merely a cover for something else? Her profile was perfect, and if you discounted the makeup and the hair, she probably could be beautiful. She had a small, straight nose, nicely shaped lips and a rounded chin, all in an oval face.

The blare of a horn signaled Randall's dalliance at a traffic light. He pushed the car into gear, cursing his momentary inattentiveness.

FRANCESCA'S MIND HAD BEEN wandering, also. She was angry with her brother. When they got through this—*if* they got through this—she was going to make him wish that he had never taken the tape. But could she blame him? If it had been her heart and soul poured into words and music, would she have acted differently? The tape, to Michael, was like a child, one he had nurtured and needed to protect. He took that duty seriously, just as she took her duties as his older sister seriously. It didn't matter that they were both adults now. When Michael needed her, she would be there for him.

In physical terms, their genes had matched only in the color of their eyes. Where her hair was fine and blond like their mother's, his was a medium chestnut with a strong inclination to curl as their father's had. She was the smallest in the family at five foot one, whereas Michael was the tallest at nearly six feet.

Growing up, they had been extremely close, as close as a brother and sister could be. They were friends with little rivalry. Possibly that was due to the fact that they had moved so often when they were small. The family was always moving from one of their father's work projects to the next. Sometimes, they truly had been each other's only friend. Then after their father's death, their mother had settled the tiny family near Sacramento on her own father's almond farm. At twelve and ten respectively, the two children had again clung together. That was especially true when their grandfather came looking for someone to blame for whatever had gone wrong on a particular day. They had learned when to hide and when to escape. Notably, they had learned how to escape into their minds when arguments raged between their mother and grandfather. Francesca had entered the world of books and ideas. Michael had turned to music.

"Where are we going?" she demanded now. She didn't like not being in command of the situation. She had to reassert control.

"The home of a friend of mine. He's away on an extended trip."

"How long will he be away?"

"Another week. Why?" Randall asked, suddenly suspicious. "Surely this won't last that long."

"I have no way of knowing."

"We should call the police."

"No!"

"I'll do all that I can to help your brother. If what you say is true, he—"

"Do you think the police can do anything more than we can? If my brother's friends won't talk to me, do you really think they'll talk to them? It's a closed world we're dealing with here. One that's very suspicious of outsiders. If word got around that the police were snooping because we had called them—"

"What about the Masseys? Will they do it?"

"You mean, will they call the police?" She laughed shortly. "No. They want them involved even less than I do."

"But if your brother took something from them that they consider is partly theirs..."

"They'll handle it in their own way. Why do you think I'm so worried?"

He made no reply. A moment later, he asked, "What are we going to do?"

"Keep talking to people."

"Which people?"

"Anyone who knows Michael."

"Does he have a backup group, a band?"

"Yes."

"Which you've already questioned?"

"I've talked to most of them."

"And?"

"And...nothing. They don't want to get involved."

"But they are involved, aren't they?"

"They're afraid."

"And you're not?"

"No." Francesca's fingers curled at the lie. She couldn't admit it, but she was. Especially when she remembered how panicked Michael had sounded when she'd talked to him last. His panic had spread to her, and it was still with her, controlled only by necessity.

As they topped a small hill and then rolled down, Francesca could see that they had drawn nearer to the bay. In the distance, spotlights highlighted the double towers of the Golden Gate Bridge, while across the bay, lights from scattered communities twinkled in the night. The car soon turned onto flat residential streets where tightly packed rows of houses lined either side.

A moment later, Randall Peters turned into an abbreviated drive and was soon ushering her inside one of the houses. Unmistakably Victorian in architecture, it had the closed feel a house collects when left untended for even a short period of time.

"I'll put the car away and be right back," Randall said before he disappeared into the recesses of the house.

Francesca's wait was uncomfortable. She sensed rather than heard the garage door on the level below open and slide shut.

Before Randall returned, she forced herself to go into the sitting room, turn on a light and start to examine some of the room's contents, as if she had every right in the world, an action that played into her desire to seem brashly confident.

He found her looking at a tiny brass dog that had been positioned on the mantel.

"Nice," she said approvingly. "Is it hand carved?"

"I don't know."

She trailed her fingers over the lacy brass fireplace fan. "Very nice," she said of the room at large. "I like it. This definitely is an improvement over the hotel."

"I'll tell Paul you approve," Randall murmured dryly.

"Is that your friend's name?"

He nodded.

She moved to the rolltop desk that dominated a corner of the room and skimmed the titles of a collection of books lining a nearby shelf. "He has good taste in reading material, too."

"I'll be sure to tell him." His tone was growing testier as he became impatient with her small talk. She had pushed him about as far as she could without driving him over the edge.

Francesca turned away from the desk to face him. "I've thought about it. Tomorrow, we should pay a visit to the person you talked to tonight. The person Susan said to call. It was a man, right?"

Randall nodded.

"Possibly he didn't tell you everything that he knew. Possibly he's trying to protect her."

"I seriously doubt that."

"Why?"

"Because he sounded disinterested. As if he couldn't care less."

"That kind of thing can be deceptive. He didn't know you."

"I told him I was Susan's brother."

"And he's supposed to believe you?"

Randall stopped arguing. It galled him to admit it, but she had a point.

"Do you still have the number you called? Did you write it down?" she asked.

"No, but I remember it."

"It's still on the message tape," she murmured. "Just in case."

"I said I remember it!"

She looked at him curiously. "Are you telling the truth?"

"Why would I lie?"

She shrugged. "No reason, I suppose."

"Thanks." He was getting testy again. His long body was beginning to sag with fatigue.

"Your friend wouldn't happen to have a reverse telephone directory, would he?" She chanced another question.

"I'm sure he wouldn't."

"Too bad. That means a stop at the library."

"Tomorrow," he said.

"Tomorrow," she agreed.

Randall continued to look at her. She seemed at home in any situation. Being in a strange place with a man she didn't know didn't seem to bother her. Perhaps she had a black belt in karate and could defend herself without raising a sweat!

He was at a loss about what to do next. He knew what he wanted to do: part of him wanted to fall into bed and pretend that none of this had happened. He wanted to pretend that Susan was safe in Paris, spending money like water. Overspending was a bad habit she'd gotten into since reaching her majority in March and receiving control of her inheritance. The first thing she'd done was go out and buy that car. The second was to throw a party for all her friends, a party he had missed because he'd been in Los Angeles attending a business meeting. If he hadn't missed the party, might he have met Michael James? he wondered. And if he had, might he have been able to intervene, to get Susan to see reason? But he doubted it because when Susan got an idea into her head, there was no stopping her. They were a little too uncomfortably alike in that respect, too. And if she thought she loved Michael James, it didn't surprise Randall in the least that she would return to Michael's side, no matter what the danger. The other part of him wanted to... The idea wasn't fully formed yet, but it had something to do with his companion. He became aware that she was looking at him expectantly, as if waiting for a reply.

"I didn't mean to tax your thought processes," she said dryly. "Let me rephrase my question. Does this house include a bedroom?"

Randall blinked, slightly embarrassed at being caught inattentive. "Yes, of course," he said. "Two, as a matter of fact."

"Then why don't we find them and make use of them. I'm tired, you're tired, and tomorrow's going to be a very long day."

Randall was spurred into action. He headed for the stairs off the entryway. "Up here. Paul's bedroom is the larger of the two. Or rather, Paul and Allison's. They've only been married for a few months. Before that, Allison used the other room for a time before she and Paul—" He stopped. He was telling this woman things she didn't want or need to know, things his friends might not appreciate a stranger being privy to. "Allison's grandfather used the guest room after they married . . . up until a couple of months ago, when he died. He didn't die in it, though, so you don't have to feel strange or anything."

"I wouldn't feel strange."

"No, I suppose not." Randall glanced at her. At times, she looked so small and fragile, which proved that appearances could be totally deceptive. He stopped at the door and motioned her inside. She went in with no hesitation. He watched as she studied the room.

Allison had erased the last vestiges of equipment that had been needed for the care of an invalid: the hospital bed, the daybed for the nurse's use, the various supplies that had increased as her grandfather's condition worsened. All that remained now, as a loving reminder of her grandfather, was the painting of a ship weathering a violent storm, which had been his favorite, and a photograph of the two of them together, taken when Allison was a teenager and her grandfather a crusty-looking old man with a slight twinkle in his eye.

Frankie went directly to the photograph, lifting the silver frame, then she put it down again without comment. She turned to test the bed's springiness, trying it with her hand. "This is fine," she said, straightening. When Randall made no move to leave, china blue eyes met his. "I said this is fine. Do you have a problem with that?"

Randall shook his head.

"Then . . . ?"

Did she sense the direction of his wayward thoughts? But if she did, how could he explain? How could he tell her that she mesmerized him? That for someone who was accustomed to doing things in certain patterns, with certain people, she was so completely out of the mainstream as to be riveting. That he had never met anyone like her!

Mentally, he ran for cover. "I was just wondering . . . your suitcase. We left it in the car. Would you like me to get it for you?"

Frankie eyed him suspiciously. Instinct must have told her that he wasn't saying everything that was on his mind. "Sure," she said. "That would be great."

Randall continued to fight against the attraction he felt for her. The bed was so close. What would she do if he . . . She was coming toward him! Did she feel the same overwhelming rush of attraction that he did? His breathing quickened. His body came alive.

She veered toward the door, held it open and waited pointedly for him to leave. "Thanks" was all she said.

Cold water wasn't delivered only from a tap.

Randall quickly escaped from the room.

LATER, ALONE in his bedroom, or rather in Paul and Allison's bedroom, Randall paced. It was ridiculous to feel this way—to be embarrassed and ashamed when he had *done* nothing! He hadn't wrestled her to the bed or ripped off any of her clothing. Except in his mind, his conscience corrected.

Susan. He had to keep his thoughts on Susan, not let them stray to other, more dangerous threats to his peace of mind. He had to keep telling himself that the only reason he was involved in this case was to help his sister out of the mess she now found herself in. *And he had to believe it!*

He continued to pace until sheer exhaustion rendered him helpless. Then after locating a towel, a spare robe of Paul's and some spare underwear, he headed down the hall toward the bathroom.

By now, he was so tired that if she came out of her room wearing nothing but bells and a smile, he wouldn't care.

Well, maybe he wouldn't care.

Chapter Five

Randall was aware of nothing until the next morning when a woman's voice urged, "You can't sleep all day. We have things to do!"

Randall slowly turned to see someone he didn't recognize standing in the doorway. This person's hair was long and dark and curled loosely to her shoulders; her head was covered by a short-brimmed, floppy hat. The rest of her clothing fit loosely, too. A loose blouse was topped by a patterned vest. A skirt, flounced and long, fell to her soft suede boots. A multitude of chains jangled around her neck and fake coins dangled from her ears. She might have been a Gypsy come straight from a Hollywood sound stage.

"Wha—" was his first attempt at language.

The dimple came and went.

"Have trouble waking up early, do we?" she taunted.

Yesterday came rushing back like an out-of-control truck. Randall winced. It was then that he realized he was wearing only a pair of Paul's designer briefs and that the cover he had once pulled over him had been kicked off. Most of his body was naked to the world!

He was unsure whether to be relieved or insulted when she calmly said, "The used-clothing store opens in fifteen minutes. We should be there."

He dragged respectability over his lap as he sat up, a hand rubbing his bleary eyes before attempting to tame the tangle of his hair. "What happened to you? You look—"

"Different?" she supplied. "Thanks. That's exactly what I want."

"I mean *really* different." Had she darkened the color of her skin, too, or was he just imagining it? It was now more of a bronze than a cream. And her skin tone made her eyes seem even more arresting. "How did you—"

"It's one of my many talents. Are you going to sit there all day?"

Normally Randall was a fairly early riser, but not after a day like yesterday, a portion of which was her fault! "Perhaps what I need is a little privacy," he snapped, not meaning to sound quite so pompous.

Again the dimple appeared. "Diffidence in a man. How quaint."

With a low growl, Randall threw the cover from his hips, stomped over to the closet where he had carefully hung his suit the night before, jammed his feet into his slacks and buttoned and zipped the fly before looking at her defiantly. Her amusement had not lessened. "You don't mind if I have a minute alone in the bathroom, do you?" he asked stiffly.

She inclined her head, after which he grabbed one of Paul's clean shirts. Fortunately they wore the same size. He walked stiltedly to the bathroom, where he leaned against the marble countertop and stared at himself in the mirror, wondering what he had ever done to deserve *this*.

He ran a hand over the light stubble on his jaw and chin, debated whether to shave, then decided to hell with it! If she could look scruffy, so could he.

RANDALL HAD NO IDEA QUITE how scruffy he could look until he stood with her in the secondhand clothing store and waited like a frozen model while she found first one bit of clothing then another. She sized the items with her eyes before holding them up against him. The stack in his arms began to grow. Shirts, pants and a jacket. There was even a pair of shoes: biker boots with chains swinging freely in the space between the sole and the heel. For a time, Randall was incapable of speech, then he burst out, "You've got to be kidding! I'm not going to wear any of this!"

China blue eyes turned on him. "You will if you want to help Susan."

Randall's irritation did not abate. "I still think that this is someone's idea of a joke. What are you going to do, get me all dressed up in this stuff and then spring the surprise? It's as good as Halloween! Only no one's going to get any treats!"

She held up a fringed suede jacket that looked like a refugee from the sixties. "Yes. I like this better than that other one. Here. Let me change it."

Randall tossed the entire bundle onto a table. "There. You can have it all. I don't want it." A street person perusing merchandise by the door moved quickly aside as Randall stalked out of the building.

Frankie caught up with him on the front sidewalk. She made a grab for his arm, holding him back. "I know you don't like the idea of dressing in these clothes. Do you think *I* do? But this is the only way! Believe me. I'm not doing it for fun." Another time, maybe. But not now. They had to wear these costumes to fit in, to not draw attention to themselves in the counter-culture world in which they had to move. Under normal conditions, Francesca took a certain pride in looking neat and well turned out. Her taste was not flamboyant. But she was doing what she had to do now in order to achieve an end. And she had to make Randall see that he did, too.

Beneath the floppy hat, her face held the appeal of a street urchin—pleading yet proud; in need, yet fiercely independent. She looked up at him, both asking for and demanding his understanding.

The strong physical appeal she held for Randall washed over him once again. The blue eyes, the oval face, the perfect body in delicate miniature. Only now he began to see the shadow of vulnerability that lay hidden beneath the hardened front she wore. He felt himself begin to weaken.

She was quick to take advantage of his vacillation. "It should only be for a few days," she pressed. "Then, when it's over, when everyone's safe, you can forget that it ever happened. No one you know will see you dressed like this, except possibly Susan. And she won't care."

Randall let himself be pulled back into the store and to the table holding his prospective wardrobe. He looked at the mound and removed the sixties jacket. "I won't wear this." Each word was enunciated with perfect precision.

"All right," she said, tossing the jacket onto another table. "That's easily taken care of." Then she gathered the remaining assortment of clothes, brought it to the cashier and paid for it with her own money, a fact that very much surprised him.

True to what she had said the night before, Frankie insisted on driving. She slid easily into place behind the wheel of the Civic and settled into the seat as if it were made especially for her. Before starting the car, she took a moment to give another careful look around. She seemed to live watching over her shoulder. Seeing no one suspicious, she said, "We're still alone, I think."

"Except for our little friends in the back seat," he contradicted.

She turned to the back seat, saw the clothes, and immediately understood what he meant. "Why are you so fixated on bugs?" she challenged.

"Because I don't care to become infested."

"Good," he said. "But I don't want to wear someone else's clothes."

"You're very fastidious."

"Very," he agreed.

"Then you'll be happy to know that the owner of this shop cleans everything before she sells it."

"How do you know?"

"I know!"

"Maybe that's not good enough."

"Would you like to stop at a Laundromat? We can do that. It will only take...oh, two or three hours out of the day. Hours we could certainly use doing something else."

Randall firmed his jaw and said nothing.

She continued to watch him, pointedly waiting for a reply she knew that he would not make. Then she explained, "I know, because I know the owner. Personally. She's a very responsible woman. I've worked with her before."

"Doing what?" Randall snapped.

Francesca frowned. "Just some stuff. Does it matter?"

"A mystery woman. You've done a little of this, a little of that. Is there anything that you *can't* do?"

"Find my brother!" she snapped before swiveling to start the engine.

The Civic roared into life, as much as it could roar. Then in a gesture of sympathy to its beleaguered owner, it promptly stalled.

"Your car's just like you," Francesca muttered almost to herself.

"Did you say something?" He had heard what she'd said, but he wanted to see if she'd repeat it.

"I said that your car's in just as foul a mood as you are!"

Extremely proud of both his and his transport's temperament, Randall said, "Neither of us are happy when forced."

"What about breakfast? Would that help?"

The way to a man's heart . . . or perhaps, was she thinking to soothe a savage breast with food instead of music? The idea worked. When he considered it, Randall suddenly realized that he was starving. He had eaten very little while traveling yesterday. He'd been too riled most of the time to want sustenance then. Now he did.

"You can change in the restroom," Francesca suggested, marring the dawning brightness of his expression.

As they drove to a café, Randall had no trouble maintaining his fierce frown. It was easy in the face of her satisfied smile.

RANDALL STARED AT HIMSELF in the cramped mirror of the café's men's room. Great heavens, what a sight! Surely she didn't expect him to present himself in public in this getup! He wore tight black pants that rode low on his hips, a lavender poet's shirt made of simulated silk with the first button nearly halfway down his chest, and the biker boots . . . He looked like something from a low-budget horror movie. All he needed was an elongated pair of fake teeth!

A tap sounded on the door. "We need to keep moving!" his tormentor called.

He shook his head, unseen. "I'm not coming out. Not like this."

"No one will notice. Not if you don't call attention to yourself."

She was right. San Franciscans were accustomed to just about everything. But he wasn't.

"*I'll* notice," he countered.

"It's necessary," she said firmly. "Now come on. We don't have all day."

"No."

"I'll have the manager make you come out."

"Go ahead and try." Why did he always feel so ridiculous when he was around her? And now he was even starting to act ridiculous.

Randall heard Frankie give an impatient sigh. That was just before she surprised him by barging into the room, her expression showing her irritation that he had forced her hand. Then slowly her irritation changed to amused appreciation as she took in the result of her handiwork.

"You look—" she began to say, but stopped.

Randall stood there, feeling like an idiot. "Silly? Ridiculous? Absurd?" he supplied.

"I was going to say perfect, but you're not. It's your hair."

Randall took a step back, as much as the tiny room would allow. "Don't touch my hair."

She ignored him, reaching out to inspect his light brown hair. Her fingers ruffled the sides, disturbed the top and still she looked dissatisfied.

"What you need is a little more body," she decided, digging into her purse for a container and a comb. She smeared some goo onto her hands, then rubbed it into his hair, not letting the fact that he tried to evade her reach give her any pause in the least. "Come here," she directed, pulling him toward the hand-drying machine near the sink. "Now bend over."

"I will n—"

She poked him lightly in the stomach and he bent.

Then she pressed the knob that controlled the emission of hot air and used the comb to best advantage. A few moments later, she was done. "There!" she said, rinsing her hands while looking at him with a little more approval.

Randall hesitated to look at himself in the mirror. When he did, though, he was surprised. She hadn't done anything too outrageous. He had meant to get his hair cut before his trip to Chicago but had gotten busy and had put off the appointment until after his return. His hair was a little longer than he usually wore it, and all she had done was persuade it to look fuller, less buttoned down, and had encouraged its inclination to curl.

"You should wear it like that all the time," she commented. "It looks good on you."

He could have agreed, but he didn't, purely because he was determined to be purely ornery. He would remember that poke in the stomach for a long time. "I liked it as it was," he said.

She shrugged. Then frowning again, she murmured in speculation, "Could we possibly pierce one ear?"

"Absolutely not!" His roar could have been heard in the café proper and probably was.

"All right. All right. Don't get so upset."

Randall breathed fire. "You tell me not to be upset! Do you have any idea of exactly how *upset* I am?"

"I have a vague idea," she murmured.

"Vague?" Randall thundered.

He was just about to really lay into her when the manager of the café poked his head around the door. When he saw that a woman was in the men's room, the manager frowned his disapproval and said, "I don't allow any funny business in my place. If you two know what's good for you, you'll get out. Before I call the police."

"B-but—" Randall stammered, mortified by what was taking place.

"Now!" the manager said. He held the door open, ordering them to leave.

Under his watchful eye, Randall collected the slacks, shoes and shirt he had discarded and followed Frankie from the room. She didn't look in the least disturbed. Her head was high, her chin up. Randall imagined that everyone was looking at them as they filed past the booth where they had eaten breakfast, paid their bill and were escorted out the door.

Walking across the tiny parking lot to the car, the morning sun revealed Randall to the world in all his glory. He dove into the passenger seat as soon as he could. He didn't even think to challenge Frankie's continued determination to drive.

Francesca watched her companion with amusement. He was exhibiting typical male behavior: trumpeting his displeasure at being forced to do something he didn't want to do while, at the same time, trying to hide from everyone's view.

She darted another glance at him as she slipped behind the wheel. He might think that he looked silly—and he would to anyone who thought that people should be slotted into narrow, confined, preconceived compartments—but he also managed to look amazingly attractive. Which wasn't surprising when you considered that he was attractive to start with. His features were clean-cut, his body lean and fluid. She remembered vividly the picture he'd made that morning stretched out in the oversize bed. His long muscles had been covered by smooth, golden skin that was, in turn, covered with a light layer of masculine hair. The hair on his chest became thicker, slightly darker, and trailed down a narrow path along his flat stomach until...

Francesca applied a screeching halt to her thoughts. She had denied them this morning, and she would deny them now. He was a nice-looking man. Full stop. There could be nothing more. At least, not while she was so intent upon helping Michael. Later? No, not even later. She'd already tried that once. She wasn't about to do it again. Not for a long time. If ever.

She concentrated on pulling out of the parking lot and onto the city street, all the while keeping an alert eye out for trouble. She knew the Masseys' flunkies would be looking for them. She only hoped it would take them a long time to catch up.

"I have to check in with my office," Randall said. It was a clipped statement, allowing no argument. "They're expecting me."

From somewhere, he had found his glasses. They were now resting determinedly on his nose. But instead of taking away from his look, they added to it, making him appear even more sexy.

"There should be a pay phone at the library," she offered.

His agreement was a quick nod.

He was still angry with her. Livid. Maybe she shouldn't have been so quick to choose all the clothing herself. But if she had waited for him to do it, it would never have happened. And if forced, he would never have picked the look he had now or any of the other looks. He would have rummaged until he found a less-natty version of the suit he had worn last night. And she had to make him fit in! "I've been thinking," Francesca said after a moment, hoping to divert his mind to other things. "We need a telephone number where we can be reached. Somewhere secure where Michael or Susan can feel it's safe to leave a message. Somewhere—'' she paused ''—like your office.''

His attention turned fully on her. "Are you completely mad?" he asked.

She pressed on. "Think about it. What better place? Your building has a security system, doesn't it? So it would be hard to get someone in there to bug it. And you have a secretary to take messages." She suddenly frowned. "What about at night? Do you have an answering service or something?"

"I have a service after hours, yes," he answered stiffly.

"Then this is what we'll do—we'll give your number to everyone we talk to. We won't tell them who you are. We'll just tell them to call if they learn anything or if they make contact with Michael or Susan. And they could call, too. It's the only way that makes sense. I was going about it all wrong before. No one was going to *tell* me where Michael is at this stage of the game. The contact will have to come from him. What we have to do is provide a bridge!"

"Have you thought about the possibility that Michael might not want you to get so deeply involved in all of this?"

"That's what Danny said, but I don't care. Michael needs me. He needs me now more than he ever has."

"Who's Danny?"

"One of the guys in Michael's band. Please." She harkened back to her earlier idea. "It's the only way."

Please? She was asking? He held his ground. "I refuse to place my secretary in any kind of danger."

"How can she be in danger?" Frankie reasoned. "All she'll do is answer the phone, just like she always does. And anyway, it's Michael the Masseys want. Michael and the tape."

"And Susan," he reminded.

"Only because she's with him."

"And you," he hazarded a guess.

Francesca shook her head vehemently. "No. They want me to lead them to him. That's the only reason I matter."

Randall took a moment to push his glasses back into place, an action that gave him time to think. "All right," he said at last. "But I'm not going to hide anything from my secretary. She gets to decide if she wants to do it. It wouldn't be fair otherwise."

It was refreshing to hear someone speak of fairness. It made up a bit for his stubborn streak. "All right," she agreed. "That's fine." She tried not to notice that he counted her capitulation as a sop to his masculine ego.

RANDALL MARCHED straight to the small bank of public telephones not far inside the library doors while Frankie went to the information desk to ask for directions to the area's telephone directories. Dressed as he was, he felt as if everyone was watching him. He didn't look around to find out.

Five minutes later, they met.

"Got it," Frankie said, brandishing a piece of paper. "It's not far from where we were earlier. It's in the Haight. What about you? Is your secretary willing to help us?"

"Yes."

"What's the matter?" she asked, looking at him curiously. "Is there another problem?"

He gave her a sour look. "Oh, no. I like to present myself as some kind of nut case to the senior partners of my law firm. I like to cause trouble for people... mess up their Fridays by making them do my work as well as their own. I also like to put people in a position where they can't say no!"

"Some people don't mind acting that way," she said.

"I'm not 'some people'!" he snapped. He took her arm. "Come on. Let's get out of here. I feel like part of a circus act."

They arrived at one of the main exit doors of the library at the same instant as a woman dressed in a designer suit, whose very upswept blond hair was perfectly in place. The look she gave Randall and Francesca when they didn't immediately hop out of the way to let her through the door first—as she seemed to think was her due—was enough to freeze the entire bay.

"Vermin," Randall heard her mutter as they finally stepped aside and allowed her to pass.

The epithet was said so tightly and with such icy disdain that for a moment, Randall was too stunned to move. Had he really heard her say that? Then anger took the place of paralysis as he realized that he had. They might not give the impression of being her social equal, dressed as they were in their oddly put together secondhand clothes, but that didn't give her the right to act superior. He started to go after her, to tell her exactly what he thought of her rude behavior. Frankie advised him not to. "Let it go," she said. "She's not worth the trouble. You'd never convince her."

"Did you hear what she said?" he demanded. He remained incredulous.

"To most people, it doesn't matter, but there's always a few who can't resist rubbing it in."

"Rubbing what in?"

"The fact that some people are different from everyone else. That they approach life from a different angle. People like her consider that terrible."

"I take it this is something you've heard before?"

Frankie scooted out the door, forcing him to follow if he wanted an answer.

"Well?" he prompted as they moved down the series of steps to the sidewalk. She could cover ground quickly. He had noticed that yesterday, and the observation was reinforced today. He had to walk fast in order to keep up.

She didn't answer until they were at the car. "Yes, I've heard it before," she said tightly. "Over and over when I was growing up, from my grandfather. But it was Michael who took it most to heart."

"What happened?" Randall asked.

When he'd wanted to be, their grandfather could be so cantankerous as to be mean. And he'd seemed to want to be mean often. He'd never approved of the idea that his grandson wanted a career in music. To him, music was a complete waste of time. Only the almond farm mattered. *Its* well-being, *its* care. And people, especially his grandson, either felt the same way or received the sharp edge of his tongue. "I don't want to talk about it," she said, her words clipped.

Randall sensed the depth of her anger and wondered at its cause. But he knew better than to probe further. In life as well as in the practice of law, discretion was often the better part of valor.

Chapter Six

The address that belonged to the telephone number Randall had called the evening before was near what was, at the height of San Francisco's hippie movement, one of the most talked about intersections in the country, Haight and Ashbury streets. Even now, the culture in the area was counter to that of other sections of the city. Aged hippies still wandered the sidewalks, manned the variety shops and hung out on the street corners. There was also a new generation that either looked sympathetically upon the hippies' philosophy or coexisted quite happily beside it. Bills posted on telephone poles still advertised every imaginable cause.

In these surroundings, Randall didn't look at all out of place. No one gave him even a long first glance, much less a second one, and he began to see the wisdom behind his companion's thinking. They walked halfway down a side street, found the address and mounted a short flight of stairs. A row of mailboxes clinging to one wall guided them to the door of the proper apartment. The aroma of frying onions was heavy in the air.

Without speaking, Frankie knocked. At the same time, she glanced at the trash collecting in the corners of the hall and the dirty, worn paint that coated—or rather, that attempted to coat—the walls.

All Randall could think of at that moment was that Susan couldn't possibly even know of a place like this, much less inhabit it. It was so far removed from her usual world as to be completely alien. The door opened to reveal a man of medium height with a huge beer belly that spilled out over the front of his pants, thinning hair and at least three days' worth of beard stubble that covered his cheeks. He had a plainly belligerent attitude. Randall's conviction that Susan had never been here deepened. Something about this wasn't right. It couldn't be right!

Before Frankie could say a word, he murmured hurriedly, "This has to be the wrong place."

The man looked from him to her. A section of newspaper hung loosely from his curled fingers. "Is that what you got me up to tell me?"

Frankie threw Randall a quelling look before gluing on a winning smile for the benefit of the man. "Are you Mr. LeBaron? Mr. Monk LeBaron?" she asked.

"And what if I am?" the man growled.

"We were wondering if we could have a word with you. Yesterday, you received a call from my friend here. He left a message with you for his sister, Susan Peters, for her to call him. Do you remember that?''

The man stepped back and started to close the door. ''I don't remember nothin', lady. Nothing' at all. Like your friend said, you've got the wrong place.''

Frankie's hand shot out. She stiff-armed the door, surprising the man by her action. ''All we want to do is talk. Ask a couple of questions. We don't want to make trouble for you or for anyone.''

''Monk?'' A woman called from inside the apartment. ''What's going on?''

The man again pushed against the door, trying to counter Frankie's delaying action. Randall added his strength to hers, keeping the door open.

The angular face of a woman of indeterminate age peeked over Monk's shoulder. ''What is it? Who are you?'' she asked.

Frankie was quick to answer. ''I'm Frankie James, Michael James's sister. I know he's in trouble and I'm trying to find him. We understand that Susan Peters was here sometime during this last week. All we want is to ask you a few questions.''

The woman studied them for a moment. ''Let them in, Monk,'' she pleaded with the intractable man. ''Quit acting like we have something to hide!''

Monk LeBaron was slow to react, but he did as the woman asked, all the while frowning with displeasure.

Inside the apartment, the smell of frying onions was stronger than in the hall, and the decor was little improved. Newspapers were strewn over a worn couch, beer bottles and overfilled ash trays littered every available surface and clothing was scattered haphazardly about.

The woman, who was rail thin and dressed in a robe, apologized. "I was making breakfast. Have you eaten? I can set two more places easy."

The invitation, extended so graciously by the woman, did not please the man. In stony silence, he walked back to the couch, plopped his considerable weight down and took another swig of beer before burying himself in the sports pages of his newspaper.

"Uh—no, no thank you. We just ate," Frankie said. "I'm sorry if we're intruding."

The woman's wan face lighted when she smiled, her washed out blue eyes coming to life. "No trouble at all," she said. "Where Monk and I were raised, hospitality comes as second nature. Somebody shows up hungry, they eat. If they need a place to stay, we find 'em a bed."

Monk snorted from behind his paper.

The woman glanced at him and motioned for her visitors to follow her into the kitchen.

"I have to stir what I'm cooking, otherwise it'll burn. That okay with you?"

The kitchen was surprisingly clean, making it obvious that Monk rarely entered it.

"Would you like a cup of coffee?" the woman asked. "My name's Anne, just so's you know. I'm

Monk's wife. We've been married ten years now. Ten years last January."

"Yes, thank you," Frankie said. Then glancing at Randall, who gave an imperceptible nod, she added, "We'd both be grateful."

"Just sit yourselves down at the table and I'll pour you a cup."

Anne lifted the lid from a fry pan, stirred the concoction within and lowered the gas flame a degree. "Monk loves fried onions with his eggs. That and lots of catsup. Now, let me get that coffee."

"We wouldn't want to delay Monk's breakfast," Randall said, speaking for the first time. There was irony to his tone, but the woman was not aware of it.

She laughed. "Oh, he can wait a few minutes. Burn a little of his blubber off." She brought three steaming cups of coffee to the table and sat down. "Now, what can I do for you? If it's about Michael, I don't know a thing. All I know is that he's hiding out. And that's only because Susan told me."

Randall couldn't prevent the question, "How do you know Susan?"

The woman looked at him long and hard. Not at his manner of dress, but at him as a person. It was as if she were trying to see what was inside him. "You look like her a little bit. Something about the shape of your nose and your mouth. I met her at the Star of Hope Mission. For a time, she came there every day to help make meals for the less fortunate. I did, too."

As a volunteer or as a recipient? Randall wondered. Then he was glad that he hadn't asked.

The woman went on. "We made sandwiches together. Bagged 'em and put 'em in stacks for someone to take out to the people lined up on the street. We made sure they had some fruit and maybe a cookie or two. I like Susan. She's a very generous person."

"Yes" was all Randall could say. Susan on a bread line? Why had she never told him? Did she think that he wouldn't approve? If so, the idea dismayed him. What must she think of him if she could believe that he would be against her doing something so unselfish? Surely she knew him better than that. He was truly puzzled.

Frankie's next question intruded into his thoughts. "We understand that Susan stayed here for a couple of days. Can you tell us anything about that?" She took a quick sip of her coffee.

"Only what I said before. She said that Michael was in trouble and she needed to find him." Anne paused to examine Frankie closely. "You're Michael's sister, you say? Now, you two don't look *anything* alike, except for the color of your eyes. They're that pretty blue like you see in fancy silks sometimes. I met your brother once. He's a real gentleman."

Frankie gave a quick smile. "We're trying to find him, too," she said. "You wouldn't happen to know where—" She stopped when Anne shook her head. Frankie tried again. "Susan wouldn't happen to have told you—" Again she stopped at a shake of the woman's head. "How long did she stay here?" she finally asked.

"Two days. Well, more like one and a half. She came on a Monday afternoon and left on a Wednesday morning."

"Did she tell you where she was going?"

"No."

"How did she seem? Excited? Afraid?"

"Both."

When Frankie lapsed into silence, Randall asked, "What was she afraid of? Did she tell you?"

"Well, for Michael's safety, of course. But there was something else."

"What?"

"I don't know. She was afraid to go out of the apartment. Afraid to even look out the windows. It was like she was afraid someone would see her. She said she didn't want to get me into trouble. That's why Monk—" The woman stopped, bit her lip and looked down at the table.

Frankie prodded Randall, then said, "We have a number we'd like you to call if you think of anything more. Or if you hear from Susan, give it to her. Tell her to call us. We want to help her, Anne."

Randall reached for a pencil lying on the table and a pad of blank paper. He wrote down his office telephone number. "Call this number anytime, day or night. Someone will answer."

The woman took the slip of paper, folded it and put it safely in the pocket of her robe.

She started to speak again, but was interrupted by her husband, who had come to stand in the doorway.

"I'm hungry, Annie girl. Starvin'. How much longer are you goin' to keep yammerin' with these people?"

Frankie and Randall stood up. The woman had enough to deal with, living with this man. Neither wanted to make her life any more difficult.

"We're leaving," Randall said.

Frankie took the woman's hand and squeezed it warmly. "Thanks for everything," she said.

The woman smiled hesitantly back.

Her husband waited for them to go.

When once again they were in the hall, Frankie expelled an angry breath. "Men like that make me want to—" For once, she couldn't seem to find the proper words. Her expression was angry, her face flushed. She seemed much larger than her height, the force of her personality expansive.

"He's a real sweetheart," Randall agreed.

Frankie started down the stairs. "Well, at least it wasn't a complete waste of time. We learned something for our trouble."

"What's that?"

"Susan asked *someone* the right question. She didn't already know where Michael was. Now all we have to do is find that same someone."

Randall reached out to stop her. They were partially down the stairs, halfway from the bottom landing. "Just because she got through to him doesn't mean that we will, too. Maybe he left word for her someplace and all she had to do was collect it."

"Are you saying that what we're doing is a waste of time?"

"I didn't say that. I just don't want you to get your hopes up too—"

"Since when have you been concerned about my hopes?" she demanded, interrupting. "We didn't even know each other before yesterday. And personally, that's just the way I'd like it to remain." She didn't *want* to get to know him. She didn't want him to get to know her. They weren't together to have fun or to explore each other's personalities. The less they knew about each other, the better things would be. That way, there would be no complications to have to deal with later. No pain.

This was the first time Randall had been dismissed quite so summarily by a woman. Not for cause, but merely because she didn't like him. The hairs on the back of his neck rose. "If things are going to get personal between us, we might as well quit right now," he returned tightly. "Go our separate ways. I'm still not convinced that we're going about this correctly. My instinct still tells me to let the authorities handle it."

"And your instinct could get them killed! I've told you that before! More than once!"

"And your way is safer? I don't see how. We don't know what we're doing. Neither one of us is experienced in detective work."

"Speak for yourself!" she snapped.

Randall groaned. "Oh, no. Don't tell me. You've done that, too! Next, you're going to tell me you're an astronaut or that you're the first woman president of the United States. Pull my other leg, would you!"

"I worked for a private investigator once," she claimed.

"Doing what? His filing?"

"A person can pick up a lot over the course of a summer!"

"How to catch a fish, yes! But not how to catch potential murderers!"

"Do you have a better idea?" she demanded. "And don't mention the police again!"

Randall thought for a moment. "I could hire an investigator."

"You're only saying that because you're afraid. Because the deeper we become involved in this, the more afraid you are. I knew you didn't want to do this. Not from the first moment I mentioned it to you."

"Mentioned!" he echoed. "I was *kidnapped!*"

"Well, no one's stopping you now! You can leave anytime you want. I'll go on with this myself. I don't need you!" She stamped down several more steps. "Men! Promise you one thing...do another. A woman can't rely on a thing one of them says."

Randall crashed after her. Pulling her back around, he thundered, "I never renege on a promise!"

Her blue gaze was infuriated. "It looks like you just did!"

Randall's fingers tightened on her arm. He wanted to shake her again. To make her see sense. Then suddenly his mood underwent a drastic change. Exactly as had happened once before, he wanted to kiss her. Only this time, unbelievably, the urge was even stronger. So strong that he couldn't resist.

Even as she started to berate him again, he swooped, drawing her close, his mouth finding and then claiming her own. Everything around them seemed transformed as if by magic. They were no longer standing in a substandard apartment building in which the tenants changed with the first of each month, on stairs that creaked under the lightest weight and under a ceiling lamp that gave far too little illumination.

Randall was ignorant of everything but the surging sensations that clamored through his body, intoxicating him. Her lips were indescribably soft and warm. Her body was palpitating. She tasted of the sweetest blend of nectar and wild honey, drawing him in and making him want to erase any roadblock to further intimacy.

She jerked away, gasping for breath, and looked at him as if he had suddenly gone mad.

Randall pulled back. He was deeply shocked! It all seemed part of some kind of fantasy. Had it happened? But he could see by the stunned incredulity of her reaction that it had, and on his own lips, he could still taste a lingering sweetness.

"Is this your way of not getting personal?" she demanded, a feral light coming into her eyes. "Because if it is—"

Randall could think of nothing to say. Such rashness wasn't a part of his nature. At least it hadn't been until he'd met her.

She watched the blood rise slowly in his cheeks, embarrassment at what he had done finding a physical release. And oddly, her anger lessened. She said, "Let's just not forget what we're trying to do here, okay? That is, if you're still willing—"

He still wanted to kiss her! Even in the midst of the present situation, once wasn't enough. But he held himself in check. "Yes. All right," he said gruffly, ready to agree to anything to salvage the situation.

Her unusual eyes roamed his face. He couldn't tell whether she had hated his touch or hated the surprise of it. For a moment though, while he was kissing her, he had felt her respond. He was sure he had.

She gave a tight nod, pulled away and covered the distance to the door. Outside, they walked down the sidewalk in silence, neither much inclined toward conversation.

The silence lasted until they were in the car. For a moment, she sat still. He wondered what she was thinking. Something about him? Something about the moment they had just shared?

Then she said, "There's one member of the band I haven't talked to yet. This person doesn't live in the city. Why don't we start there? The others, we'll catch tonight, one by one if we have to. Most of them have jobs playing at different clubs. They're good, so they're in demand."

He was surprised at how disappointed he felt. How quickly she seemed to have put all thought of their kiss out of her mind! She was so centered on what they had to do. He was, too. He was concerned for Susan, but his every conscious thought wasn't about her. "And this guy's not?" he asked, following up on what she had said.

She laughed. "Oh, this person's good, all right. One of the most promising bass guitar players in the Bay Area. At least, that's what Michael says. But he's a she. She's just had a baby, so she's not on the circuit. That's what she was doing when I tried to talk to her earlier this week."

"Having a baby?" Randall echoed.

She nodded. "Four days ago."

"Good—" He had been going to say "grief," but the word never made it past his lips. Something caught his eye on the street. The sleek, black Cadillac was almost directly across from them in the far left lane of traffic. It proceeded very slowly, as if to give the thugs inside ample opportunity to examine the sidewalk's population.

Frankie followed the direction of Randall's startled gaze and gave a small gasp. She turned quickly away. "Get down!" she hissed.

"Where?" he shot back.

"Down there!" She indicated the footwell of the Civic.

"I can't—"

She attempted to help him by folding him forward at the waist and pushing on his back. But no amount of pushing would work. It was physically impossible for him to crumple his length into the small space. But he did keep his head down, out of view, trying not to be aware of the strain. He was conscious that she had become very still. He twisted until he could see that she was leaning against the door rest, shielding her cheek with her spread fingers while she used the brim of her hat to obscure the rest of her face.

Time seemed to expand. Seconds filled with thousands of milliseconds. Finally she touched his shoulder. "It's okay. They're gone. But we'd better get out of here. They might come around the block again."

He straightened slowly, his cramped muscles protesting. "Did they recognize us?" he asked.

"They wouldn't be gone if they had. The wig worked. So did the car. It was a good idea."

A compliment? He hadn't expected that.

If he expected her to make another quick getaway, he was again nonplussed by her contradictory behavior. They left the curb as sedately as a minister might.

And just as quietly, they blended in with the other cars on the street, instantly lost to prying eyes.

The sideways glance he gave her contained the first grains of admiration. Maybe she really did know what she was doing, after all. Maybe some lessons from that summer she claimed to have spent working in an investigator's office actually had rubbed off.

For the first time, Randall felt a small spurt of optimism.

Chapter Seven

The bass guitarist didn't play in a band because she needed the money. Not from the looks of the house she lived in in the far East Bay, outside the city. Perched high on a hillside that overlooked the entire Diablo Valley and surrounded at appropriate distances by other houses of the same quality, the cedar-and-glass structure took best advantage of the million-dollar view.

The landscaped yard, the circular drive, the brick walkway leading to the front door—all spoke of a high degree of financial security. So did the decor inside the house... and the maid.

"Miss Jessica asked me to tell you that she'll be with you in a moment," the maid said, showing them into the living room.

They waited on a white, leather couch. A huge painting of a peacock, its tail spread to full glory, dominated the opposite wall. Rich color accents resonated throughout the room, picking up the hues of the peacock's tail, which was splashed against basic white. Even the rug was of a shaggy white material. It was spread on a highly polished wood floor. Not a speck of dust was allowed to settle, glass gleamed, and strategically placed plants spread their branches with just the right artistic bent.

Randall lifted an eyebrow in appreciation. "She has good taste," he murmured to his companion.

"I'll be sure to tell her you approve," Frankie returned, mimicking his reaction to her similar statement about Paul and Allison's home.

He knew immediately what she was doing. "You have to admit, after what we saw earlier..."

"You can't tell anything about a person just by looking at them or by where they live. You have to go deeper. See inside them."

"What do you see when you look inside me?" he asked, curiosity compelling him.

Those beautiful eyes turned on him. She belonged in a setting like this, he thought. She was beautiful and softly exotic, like some kind of spoiled jungle cat. A cat with china blue eyes.

"I don't know," she said after a moment. "I haven't figured you out yet."

"I'm not all that difficult," he said. "What you see is basically what you get."

She shook her head in disagreement. "No. No one's like that. Not one person in the world. All people have secrets."

He looked at her inquisitively. "You seem to specialize in secrets. Why?"

She stood and walked over to one of the long windows. She seemed to be contemplating the view of the populated valley. But Randall could tell that her mind was elsewhere. What was she thinking? he wondered. Was there something besides love that motivated the fierceness of her determination? He voiced a speculation. "Is it because you're afraid to trust anyone?"

She whirled to face him. "Stop trying to analyze me, okay? You're not a shrink, and I'm definitely not your patient."

"But I could be your friend," he said quietly, surprising himself as much as he surprised her.

Her lips curled with mockery. "That's not the relationship you seemed to want earlier."

She had him there. He had wanted more...much more. And he still did. Everything about her intrigued him. The way she tilted her head when listening, the way she moved her hands, the graceful way she walked, and the touch of sadness in her gaze when she didn't know she was being watched.

"I can turn around and forget I heard that, or I can stay and try to hear more...." A husky voice entered their exchange.

Randall turned to see a slender woman, somewhere in her latter twenties, dressed in tight, leather pants and a matching scarlet, leather top. Without them being aware, she had come into the room. Her artificially dark hair was cut close to her head, except for a long rattail that was bleached blond and curled loosely at the back of her neck. Her features held a pixielike quality that was emphasized by rather small, dark eyes.

She smiled with genuine amusement and announced, "I think I'll stay!"

"Jessica," Frankie said warmly.

The woman frowned, squinted, then asked, "Frankie? Is that you? Why are you wearing a wig? And why are you dressed—"

Frankie halted the growing list of questions. "That's why we've come to see you. Do you have time to talk?"

Jessica shrugged, a little self-consciously. "Actually, I thought you were someone else. When Marie said that a man and a woman were here, I assumed you were the people my husband wants me to meet. They're supposed to have some great connections that can really help my career. You know I want to sing my own stuff. They should be here anytime now, but until then . . . sure, we can talk."

"It's about Michael," Frankie explained.

Jessica lost her smile. "If I knew anything, I'd tell you. You know that. But I've been a bit in the dark lately. Having a baby kind of takes over your life."

A smile flickered across Frankie's lips. "I haven't heard. Is it a boy or girl?"

"A girl." Jessica beamed proudly. "Six pounds, three ounces, with great lungs. I think she's going to be a lead singer herself." She turned to include Randall in her smile, although her gaze was puzzled.

Frankie immediately introduced them. "This is Randall Peters. Susan's brother."

"Susan." The woman repeated his sister's name.

Randall couldn't tell at first whether she'd said it with approval or disapproval. When he finally decided that it held disapproval, he immediately wanted to jump to Susan's defense. But Frankie had already gone on, drawing the other woman's attention.

"When was the last time you saw either of them?" she asked.

"I saw Michael about three weeks ago. No, two and a half. We were at the studio, listening to one of the final versions of the tape and discussing how upset we were that the Massey brothers were taking over Glass House. Michael was really jumpy. He found fault with everything. You know how he gets sometimes. He didn't like this, he didn't like that. I was ready to hit him or something, even in my advanced stage of pregnancy. But I didn't know what he was planning to do. I don't think anyone did. Except him. The idiot." She took a breath. "I haven't seen Susan in a couple of months. She was going off on some kind of trip, wasn't she?" *Good riddance,* seemed to complete her thought, but the words remained unsaid.

Randall frowned. "You don't like her?"

Jessica shrugged. "She's all right." She looked at her watch. "I wish I could help you more, but little Jessie is going to wake up soon and I'll need to take care of her before my other guests arrive. I don't have a nanny for her yet. I thought that Marie and I could handle everything by ourselves. At least, for the first few weeks. I don't want to share her any sooner that I have to."

"I understand," Frankie said. She reached out to hug the leather-clad figure. "I'm sorry we had to bother you so soon. You look radiant. Childbirth's been good to you."

"You should see Andy. He's the proudest poppa around. He's already taken about a thousand pictures. Shows them to anyone who'll stand still long enough."

"I am going to ask you a favor, though," Frankie said.

"What?"

"If you hear from Michael, will you give him this telephone number? I want to talk to him, Jessica. There's got to be a way that we can help."

"The Masseys have to be extremely unhappy," she warned.

"I know."

"I don't want anything to happen to him, Frankie. You know I don't. I'm happy now. The past is the past. I don't hold any grudges."

Frankie squeezed her hand.

The maid came hurrying into the room from another part of the house. "Miss Jessica . . . little Jessie, she's crying."

Jessica turned away but turned back again almost at once. Looking directly at Randall, she said, "The same goes for Susan. Although there was a time—"

She stopped, saw something in the past, then roused herself to answer her future. She gave Randall a wisp of a smile before hurrying away, allowing the maid to see them to the door.

"DO I TAKE IT that Michael and Jessica were lovers?" Randall asked as the car wended its way down the steep hillside.

Frankie nodded. "For a couple of years."

"Is the baby his?"

She shot him a look. "No!"

"I wondered because I've gotten the impression that Susan and Michael haven't known each other all that long. Am I right?"

"They've known each other long enough."

"If Susan didn't break them up, why is Jessica jealous of her?"

"Have you ever been in love?" Frankie demanded. "If you had, you'd know it's not that easy to turn off."

"Is that experience talking?"

Her grip tightened on the steering wheel. She didn't seem to mind asking him personal questions, but she didn't like it at all when he asked the same of her.

He decided to continue, adopting a slightly mocking tone. "So it didn't work out. Why not? Did you order him around too much?"

"We're not talking about me."

"Funny. I thought we were."

The car swayed hard to the right then to the left as she continued to make her way a little too fast and, since his last statement, a little too recklessly down the curving roadway.

Randall gripped the seat cushion again. She noticed and gritted her teeth.

"I'm not going to kill you," she snapped.

"It's hard to tell."

"What's the matter with you? Don't you know that men are supposed to be brave?"

"Who says? And who says I'm not brave? Just because I can recognize danger when I see it doesn't mean that I'm any less of a man."

"I have everything under control."

"Everything?"

Thankfully, they had already arrived safely at the bottom of the hill. He wasn't sure that he would have taunted her so strongly if they hadn't.

She made no reply, whether because she chose not to or because she was too beside herself to speak, he never knew.

THEY LEFT THE EAST BAY by way of the Bay Bridge and after paying the toll, drove smoothly into the five lanes of traffic traveling into San Francisco. To Randall's mind, the Bay Bridge had always been more appealing than its more famous sister. The Bay Bridge was longer and more complicated, made up of different styles of construction, including cantilever and suspension. A portion even tunneled through tiny

Yerba Buena Island, which was a midway anchor for both spans. And the view was fabulous. Made up of two decks, one for traffic going east and the other for traffic going west, Randall and Frankie basked in the sun of westward travel. Randall could see the skyline of San Francisco, Coit Tower and the Golden Gate.

"What's next?" he asked, when he thought enough time had elapsed since their last verbal altercation.

"It's still too early for anyone to be at the clubs. We shouldn't get there until about ten o'clock. I was thinking that possibly we should—" A car zoomed by, cutting much too closely into their lane. Frankie had to react quickly to avoid a crash. It was a black car, a black Cadillac.

Randall sat instantly erect. "Is it them?" he asked, startled.

The expression on her face answered him without words.

"But how—" Randall sputtered.

"I don't know! They must have spotted us sometime when we didn't see them."

The black car slowed, shot forward, slowed again, the driver pumping the brakes, playing with them. Trapped on the bridge, there was nothing they could do! The black car changed lanes and dropped back until it was directly opposite them. The leering face of one of the men poked out the open window. "My, my, what a surprise! Look who we've found. And to think, we almost didn't come this way."

Frankie accelerated. The black car kept pace.

The hatchet-faced man laughed. His gaze traveled to Randall. "This the new boyfriend? He looks like a wissy to me."

Frankie hit the brakes, slid into an open spot in the next lane and tried to fit into a grouping of cars that were going more slowly.

For a moment, the black car couldn't get close. Then as they approached the tunnel, the little group of cars disbanded. Two turned off toward the Naval Installation on nearby Treasure Island. Randall saw Frankie's hand instinctively twitch, as if she, too, had been tempted to turn off. But he was relieved to find that she didn't. Where would they have gone on a tiny island?

The black car was directly behind them and seemed content to stay there for a time. Frankie changed lanes again. The black car did, too. "Hang on," she directed as they neared the far side of the bridge.

Suddenly, as soon as the bridge touched land, Frankie swung the car two lanes to the left in order to spiral down the first available exit. The speed sign said twenty miles an hour and meant it. It was like driving down a corkscrew. For once, she didn't push the limit. But when they reached street level, Frankie gunned the little engine, forcing it up to speed. She then made several dizzying turns before pulling into a protected lay-by.

Neither spoke. Their hearts pumped; breath was short. The black car never showed up. Either the driver had been unable to switch lanes on the bridge as quickly as they had and had been cut off by the press of traffic or they had lost them on the city streets. Frankie curved her arms around the steering wheel and leaned forward to rest her head.

After a moment, Randall asked, "Where did you learn to drive like that?"

"You won't believe me," she said into her arms.

"Try me."

"I once moonlighted as a chauffeur for a company that provided drivers for business executives. They made me take a course in evasive driving tactics."

"You're right. I wouldn't believe you . . . if this was the normal world. But this isn't the normal world, is it? I mean, in the normal world, people don't get chased across bridges by other cars, they don't get kidnapped and they don't wear clothes like these. Well, maybe some people do." He sighed and looked at her. When she raised her head—wig, earrings and all—she reminded him once again of a vulnerable child. "How old *are* you?" he suddenly demanded. "You can't have done all the jobs you claim and look as young as you do. I just don't believe it!"

"I'm twenty-six."

"You don't look it."

"I feel older."

Randall struggled with a mix of conflicting emotions. He was in a situation he didn't choose, exposing himself to danger, and he was doing it all to help a sister he didn't seem to know anymore. Not to mention the fact that he was wildly attracted to a woman he knew nothing about. This woman! A person who carried a chip on her shoulder at least double the size of the rock on which Alcatraz sat. He had every reason in the world to be angry, but the only sentiment he could summon at the moment was compassion. "Don't worry," he said. "We'll find your brother. Everything will work out all right."

"Sure," she said, not attempting to disguise her pessimism.

"We will!" he said encouragingly, then thought for a moment. "I have an idea. Why don't we go back to Paul and Allison's place and let me collect today's messages from my answering machine. Who knows? There might be a message from Susan. She did say she'd call when she could."

"And there is always Anne," Frankie murmured.

"That's right! She might have remembered something." He smiled, trying to cheer her. The smile he received in return remained disheartened.

THERE WAS NO MESSAGE ON the machine from Susan and no message at the office from Anne. Francesca tiredly mounted the stairs to the bedroom she had used the night before. *Slept in* was a term she couldn't use. She'd barely slept through all the long hours of darkness. Just as she had slept only fitfully since first learning that Michael had actually carried out his plan. She seemed to be existing on nerves alone.

She sat down on the comfortable bed but immediately got up to pace. This room was definitely an improvement on the crummy hotel. It was beautiful, even if it had been a sick room. But when a person was ill, wasn't that the time when beauty was needed most?

Francesca paused beside the picture in the silver frame and lifted it again for study. The teenage girl was beautiful, too, slight of build with red-gold hair, creamy skin and eyes that were either blue or green. She looked young, sweet and trusting, but there was an edge of pain to the haunting smile that she gave the crusty-looking older man at her side. The man, in turn, held her hand—lightly, comfortably—with a slight smile touching his expression.

Francesca put the picture back facedown and walked away from it. Grandfathers weren't always what they were cracked up to be. Just ask her, she knew. From looking forward to living on the almond farm with their grandfather to actively hating it had been a short jump.

She and Michael had never met their grandfather before. Their mother had been cut off by him from the day she defied him to marry their father. He had only accepted her return because of the circumstances of her husband's death and the obvious need of her children. And he never let her forget his generosity. If it weren't for him, he repeatedly said, she would be out on the street, her and her *ill-gotten litter!* And it had made no difference to him if the children heard.

To their mother's credit, she had fought against their grandfather's innuendo and outright accusations. But she was dependent upon him, so they had stayed. And all the while, their grandfather had tried to bend them to his will, not caring about the cruelty of his methods.

Francesca parted the window curtain to gaze outside. It was another beautiful evening in the city. The setting sun was warm, but tempered by a biting breeze. A child played with a dog on the sidewalk. Both the child and dog were under the watchful eye of the child's mother. Laughter caught on the breeze and was carried through the open window. Francesca smiled, remembering her own laughter and that of her brother when their father was alive.

He had loved them and cared for them to the best of his ability. He had loved their mother, too. He would never have let them be hurt by the hateful words and actions of their grandfather. Neither would he have cared what they did with their lives, as long as they didn't harm anyone and were happy.

Impatiently Francesca turned away from her memories. Time was running out. She wanted to be out there, doing something. She didn't want to lose even one moment. But going to the clubs much before ten o'clock would do no good. The people they needed to see wouldn't be there yet. Only after the promise of night had truly settled in did these people stir to life, even if they assumed other identities in the day to make a living or to go to school.

Another thing. She needed a break from Randall Peters. It seemed all too easy for him to pull her off track. Like that kiss he had delivered earlier in the day!

She didn't know why he had done it! She had been berating him, telling him to leave her alone, to let her go her own way. Then all of a sudden, he had swooped and she had been left speechless, shocked, surprised. But she also had liked it. She'd responded to him in spite of her determination not to, and even after reminding herself of Sean's duplicity. Which proved just how much of a danger he could be to her.

As if she wasn't already involved in enough danger!

Chapter Eight

The music was loud, played at highest volume. Frankie pulled Randall into the club. She was dressed in tight, black pants, a spangled blouse and her old black leather jacket. Her hair was slickly smoothed back away from her face, and she had the overdone-makeup style she'd worn when they'd first met.

Randall, too, was wearing something different. The tight black pants again, but this time with a studded leather belt, a white-ribbed undershirt, an open, black overshirt and, of course, his biker boots.

All around the small, low-ceilinged room, a mass of young people in various stages of dress and undress—some laughing and talking, some dancing—were all participants in a festival of life.

Although he was dressed in a manner that did not call attention to himself, Randall felt like an alien being in a world he didn't know. It wasn't that he disapproved of their world. It just wasn't *his* world. He was accustomed to moving in vastly different circles where three-piece suits and a stricter observance of the rules were the norm.

In marked contrast, Frankie walked ahead of him, sure of what she was doing. Gone was the touch of vulnerability she had revealed earlier in the day. When she had come downstairs ready for the night, the clear light of determination had been back in her eyes. "He's over there," Frankie said, changing direction to wend their way through the crush of tables outlining the dance floor.

She moved toward the raised platform that served as a stage and didn't stop walking until they were opposite a tall, young man of medium build, who was talking with a cluster of companions. His hair was cut in a burr, and an earring dangled almost to his shoulder, while a series of tattoos ran down one arm.

Frankie touched his tattooed arm, drawing his attention. "Danny, I have to speak with you again," she said.

Danny didn't look particularly pleased to see her. His rough-cut features remained tight even when he smiled. "Hey, Frankie. Always good to see you. But I can't help you right now, honey. I've already told you all I know."

"Maybe if we talked over there," Randall suggested, indicating a spot distant from the young man's friends.

"Have we been introduced?" Danny demanded.

"Not yet," Randall replied.

"Danny, please," Frankie said, intervening. "I wouldn't ask if it wasn't important!"

Danny leaned close to her. "If I knew where Michael was, I'd talk to him myself. Tell him to give back that damn tape. It's not worth getting hurt over. Nothing is."

"But would it end there?" Randall asked. "The Masseys don't seem to like brother Michael personally."

"Has someone threatened you, Danny? Is that why you're afraid?" Frankie asked.

"I'm not afraid," he claimed, but his denial was much too quick to be convincing.

"Danny, Michael gave you your first break. Your loyalty should be to *him*."

"Loyalty doesn't do you much good when your hands are crushed. It's hard to play keyboard in finger splints!"

"Is that what they told you they'd do?" Frankie demanded. "That they'd hurt your hands?"

Danny turned to Randall, for the first time dropping the hard edge he seemed to cultivate. "Take her home and lock her up in a closet or something, will you? Before she gets hurt, too."

"Too?" Frankie echoed faintly. "Has Michael been hurt?"

Randall felt his insides sink. The situation was again losing its surrealistic quality and becoming more real.

"No! At least, not that I know of," Danny answered.

"Susan?" Frankie quizzed, mirroring Randall's concern.

"No!"

"Then who . . ." she started to ask, but stopped.

Danny had begun to sweat profusely, not merely from the heat of the club. In response to the sudden look of comprehension that dawned in Frankie's eyes, he burst out, "Yes, me. Okay? They got ahold of me the other night, laid on a few good ones and told me to tell Michael what they had done. They nearly broke a couple of ribs! That's why I'm not playing tonight. And that's why I'm not going to talk to you any longer. If I haven't already—" He looked furtively around and slid away, leaving both them and their companions. He hadn't completed his sentence, but he hadn't needed to. He was afraid and for good reason.

Frankie refused to witness his departure. She turned to Randall, a sheen of tears glistening in her eyes. "See!" she demanded. "Now do you see why Michael is so afraid?"

"They're hoods," Randall said quietly. "They think that if they can apply enough pressure in the right places, your brother will give himself up."

"Then what would they do?"

"Probably rough him up a bit, too, to make an example of him."

"You're just guessing. They might kill him!"

"Probably not. People go to jail for things like that."

"Not if they're not caught!"

"I think you'd better be a little more careful. If they're starting on Michael's friends, you've probably jumped to the top of their list."

"I'm not afraid of them," she claimed.

"Maybe you should be."

"Here we go again!" she cried. "You want to call it off, break our agreement. Let Michael and Susan fend for themselves!"

"I didn't say that."

"But you're thinking it!"

The loud music made conversation difficult, yet they seemed to have no problem.

"What would you do if the situation was reversed? What if Michael was trying to find you?" he challenged. "Would you want him to take the chance of getting hurt?"

She looked at him angrily. "That's not fair. It's not the same thing at all."

"Yes, it is."

"So what do you want me to do?"

"Let the real professionals handle it."

"That's the lawyer in you talking," she accused.

"That's what I am. Which is why I'm involved in this mess in the first place. If I were a—a real-estate broker, you wouldn't have bothered with me for a second."

The tears of frustration that had threatened to fall a moment before could no longer be held back. They rushed into her eyes and rolled down over her cheeks.

When she looked at him, it was with such plaintive accusation that Randall felt a stab in his heart.

He started to reach out to her, to apologize, to do whatever it took to not have her look at him like that again, but it was too late. She was already hurrying away, leaving him at a disadvantage as he tried to push through a newly arriving group of people at the front door.

THE COLD NIGHT AIR HIT Francesca like a blow after the stifling heat of the club. Her tears, still streaming down her face, felt like drops of icy rain. She felt so alone. She was overwhelmed by both the course and the pace of events. If she didn't succeed, this wasn't just some family tiff that could be mended. This was Michael's life she was fighting to preserve. His very existence. And when the going got even rougher, she would truly be on her own. She couldn't count on Randall Peters. He wouldn't help her.

She looked down the street in both directions, past the cars that lined each curb. She saw traffic moving across a busy intersection several blocks away, but this particular block was quiet. She wanted to find a taxi, but realized that they probably had few calls to come to this particular area. Most of the club's patrons either drove or rode public transportation.

She started off toward the busy street. All she wanted to do was go back to the hotel. Her seedy little room seemed a safe haven at the moment. It was safe from thugs who beat up on innocent people, safe from tall, handsome men who refused to live up to expectations . . . or to their promises.

She wasn't asking that much, was she? Just for his help? And it wasn't as if she was asking for herself alone. His sister was in almost as much trouble as her brother.

Streetlights were far apart along this section of sidewalk. Pools of darkness were wide. Francesca didn't care. Her feet made a rapid tattoo; she was almost running.

Leftover tears blurred her vision. A car turned into the street. Instinctively Francesca darted into a doorway, only to disturb a man who was sleeping there. She squeaked in surprise, darting away again when he made a halfhearted grab for her. The car passed by. It wasn't a Cadillac.

With her heart thumping wildly, she continued toward the busy street. Soon, footsteps could be heard closing in behind her. She turned around to see the outline of a man. The man in the doorway? she wondered. She quickened her pace, fear of another kind tightening her throat. Useless tears again flooded her eyes, making vision difficult. The man drew close. A hand reached out. Viselike fingers slipped around her arm, jerking her to a stop. Francesca fought against him. She screamed and went for his face with her fingernails.

"Frankie!" Hands collected her hands, kept them from inflicting wounds. "Frankie, look at me!"

Her breath continued to come in short, quick inhalations. Her eyes remained half-wild. She was like a cornered animal, terrified, listening only to instinct.

Again, the voice ordered her to look at him, only this time it was more familiar, concerned, and it cut through the coldness of her fear like the warmth of a spring day.

Slowly her eyes focused. She saw him and collapsed against his chest. Her entire body shook.

Randall folded her gently into his arms, making her feel warm, welcome and safe.

She continued to tremble against him before suddenly realizing where she was. Within a second, she was pushing herself violently away. "No!" she cried, more to herself than to him.

He caught ahold of her when she tried to run away. "Frankie, stop! Where do you think you're going? What are you going to do?"

"I'd rather be anywhere than here with you!" She said it, but she didn't mean it. She could think of any number of worse places. But he'd hurt her in the club, disappointed her and let her down. Just as Sean had done when she'd found out that he'd been seeing one of her friends behind her back.

"And walk right into the hands of those two thugs?" Randall demanded angrily. "Think, Frankie."

"I don't care what you say!" She was reacting like a juvenile, but it didn't seem to matter. She didn't want to listen to reason.

"Then think about Michael!" he argued swiftly. "That's all I've heard from you since the first moment we met. Michael needs you. He needs your help! Think what effect it would have on him to know that you're being held by the Masseys. He'd give himself up in a second. Is that what you want?"

Francesca had grown confused about a lot of things, but Michael's safety wasn't one of them. Randall had finally gotten through. "No," she whispered, suspending all her efforts to escape.

"The rules of engagement have changed," he continued. "You have to watch out for yourself. It's possible that the Masseys *do* want you now almost as much as they want Michael, if for different reasons."

"Are you saying I should quit?" she flared.

Randall smiled at her rallying spirit. She saw a flash of white teeth gleam in the partial light. "No," he answered. "Just be aware of it and act accordingly."

"What about you? They could use you against Susan."

"They don't know who I am."

"They will," she promised.

"Let's hope we'll have it all settled by then. It doesn't make sense that no one knows where they are. Someone has to be helping them."

Francesca stared up at him, sensing a subtle shift in the tenor of his thinking. "You truly believe that?" she asked, her voice becoming husky.

"I truly believe it," he said.

A warmth radiated throughout Francesca at his words. The warmth of relief because she was no longer so achingly alone. She drew a halting breath.

Randall continued to look at her. She couldn't see his eyes clearly, but she knew that they were intent. Then the atmosphere between them subtly shifted and became electric. Her heart rate accelerated, only this time the cause wasn't fear.

His head and shoulders were in silhouette, but she didn't need to see his face to know what he was thinking. And if she closed her eyes, the feeling became even more intense. It was as if they were communicating on some primal level that needed no formal words.

He moved forward, pressing toward her, forcing her back against the side of the nearest building. She felt the coldness of a plate-glass window against the back of her jacket. More from habit than the lack of desire, she tried to push him away, whereupon, he gathered her wrists, one in each hand, and held them against the glass on either side of her head.

If she expected a display of hurried lust, she was pleasantly mistaken. After taking command of the situation, Randall Peters did everything slowly, deliberately. He started by placing slow, lingering kisses along the sensitive areas of her face—on her eyes, beside her ears, on the corners of her lips and on her chin. Then his lips moved down her neck to the hollow of her throat.

Francesca closed her eyes, weakness making her knees tremble. Her fingers curled around his. Her breaths became so short as to be almost nonexistent. His was a skill not learned in a moment.

He pulled back and looked at her, his gray eyes serious yet burning with a light that ignited an answering fire deep within her, making her lift her face for more. He obliged, lowering his mouth until it touched hers, tasting the sweetness of her lips, allowing her an awareness of his need.

The world with its attendant problems dropped completely from Francesca's mind. She forgot to think of where they were standing, of who might be watching and of the fact that if the situation were to go further, they would have no place for privacy. None of that mattered at the moment. For now, she had what she wanted most. His body was solidly against hers, covering her, almost shielding her. Yet he did not shield her from the potency of his desire.

The pace of his lovemaking increased, but it was still smooth, slowly advancing, allowing her to experience every nuance. He freed her hands, which automatically twined around his neck, drawing him even closer. His hands went to her waist, spreading out over the curve of her back and the flair of her hips. Still, not a word had passed between them. There were only the soft sounds of a shared need.

His hands had moved upward, sliding over the bare skin that covered her ribs—having already brushed aside the tail of her spangled blouse—when the roar of a motorcycle engine impinged upon the beauty of their universe. The loud, grating noise was enough to shatter the beauty of any world. The motorcycle raced down the street and stopped in front of the club before turning around to fly back, the driver doing a wheelie as he went.

Randall's body was taut from surprise. Francesca was trembling again, but this time, the cause was mixed. The sensations that still flooded her body pulled her one way, while her mind drew her yet another. As seconds passed, full clarity returned, seemingly for both of them. She moved away from the plate-glass window while Randall shifted his shoulders and frowned.

"That—" She tried to speak but couldn't. She tried again. "Don't—don't take that for anything more than what it was. It didn't mean anything."

He looked at her, saying nothing.

She continued to explain. "We're two adults. Things like that happen sometimes. What—what we have to see to is that it doesn't happen again."

She couldn't deny responsibility! She had wanted it as much as he had!

"If you say so," he replied, his voice sounding just as odd as hers.

She dared to look at him and was glad for the semidarkness that hid her heated cheeks. She stuffed her hands into the pockets of her jacket and started to walk, chin down, along the sidewalk toward the club. After a moment, he followed.

Francesca didn't want to return to the light, but she didn't want to stay in the dark with him, either. She was still too unsettled. The possibility was great that it could all happen again. And next time, there might not be a handy motorcycle to interrupt.

She drew an unsteady breath. She was afraid that she would never be able to look at him in the same way again. Not after knowing the exquisite way he made love. And they had barely gotten started! What would it be like to go— She immediately censored the thought, not letting herself finish it.

THEY RETURNED to the noise of the dance club. The band had shifted to another piece of music, but Randall could tell little difference. The same driving beat flowed from one song to the next, and the people talking and dancing didn't seem to notice.

Frankie led the way again, but this time, Randall was on his own. She had not sought his hand as they came in the door. Which was just as well, he considered, for the sake of his shattered equilibrium. He was always a person in control, always the cool observer. He had specialized in passing out sage advice to his clients and to his friends. But where was this sage advice now that *he* needed it? Obviously nowhere in the vicinity!

He had behaved like a rutting animal, seeing what he had wanted and trying to take it. He hadn't cared that it wasn't the civilized thing to do or who might be witness. In the space of a heartbeat, all caution had vanished. And that vision of himself was unsettling.

His attraction to Frankie was stronger than any he had ever felt for a woman before. He had sensed it from the beginning, but now, it was undeniable fact.

Was it purely sexual attraction, or was there something more? Something that was fluttering lightly, just out of reach of his grasp.

They spent another hour in the club, Frankie stopping to talk to first one person, then another, picking them seemingly at random. But her method must have held firm reasoning. Each person she talked to took one of the cards she had prepared earlier in the day with Randall's office number written on it, pocketed it and promised to pass the number on if they met someone they thought could use it. But Randall and Frankie still gained precious little information. Actually none that they didn't already know.

Randall's ears were throbbing by the time they returned to the car. Even the quiet seemed loud to him. He placed both hands over his overly sensitive ears and rubbed, shaking his head and trying to make them work properly again. "I think I should change my profession," he said a bit too loudly before quickly modulating his voice. "The world's going to need more hearing specialists than lawyers in a few years."

"You get used to it," she said. "Haven't you been to a dance club before?"

"A few, but none like that. What was that music they were playing? It sounded like—" He stopped, at a loss for words.

"It's the latest in Industrial technopop."

"Do you like it?" he asked, amazed.

"Not exactly. But I understand it. I understand what they're trying to say."

"I didn't know they were trying to *say* anything."

"Listen to the words sometime," she suggested. "To the idea the artists are trying to get across. They might surprise you."

"There were words?" he returned, feigning shock. "Is that what your brother plays?"

She shook her head. "Not exactly. His style is softer. But it would still sound strange to you if you don't like this type of music."

"I didn't say I didn't like it."

She threw him a skeptical look. It was the first time she had really looked at him since they'd kissed, and she quickly looked away. She could not afford to get emotionally involved right now. She would not!

After checking the area around them for intruders, she started the car and slipped easily out of the parking space. Across the street, a couple walked slowly down the sidewalk, arms wrapped tightly around each other, bodies touching from knee to neck. At almost the same spot in front of the plate-glass window, they stopped to share a kiss. A long, intense, uninhibited kiss that seemed to last forever. Both Francesca and Randall saw them. Francesca's hands convulsed. Randall felt his stomach wrench. As Randall's car rolled by, the couple on the sidewalk remained blissfully unaware.

Chapter Nine

The next club they entered proved to be just as loud and just as crowded as the first. The feel of the place, though, was different. The attitude was calmer, the people less brittle. Several members of Michael's group were working here and Francesca and Randall waited for them to take a break.

Randall liked this music better. The decibel level remained just as earsplitting, but the music's edge was a little less intense.

"I've heard that Marc saw Michael a few days ago," the last band member they talked to said. His dark hair was cut with military precision, matching in style the short army jacket he wore that had faded decorations still attached. Except for the fact that hair growth was discouraged on all but the very top, he looked fairly normal. And barring the baggy, black pants that hugged only his ankles, he might even have passed inspection.

"Marc?" Randall echoed.

Frankie tried to contain her excitement. "Lead guitar," she answered, not bothering to explain further. "Where is he? Is he here?"

The musician shook his head. "He's been sick for a few days. Some kind of flu, I guess, although it's a little early for that."

"Where does he live? We'll want to talk to him."

The musician became wary. "I don't think I should tell you that."

"Billy, please! This is for Michael!"

"Marc won't like it." Billy wrestled with his conscience, then the appeal in Frankie's face won out.

With equal portions of both satisfaction and irritation, Randall saw that other men found her just as difficult to resist as he did.

"Oh, all right," the young man groaned. "But don't tell him I'm the one who told you." He gave them an address. "He should be there now, unless he's lying about being sick."

Frankie smiled. "Thanks, Billy. I won't forget this."

Billy shot Randall a speculative look, as if wondering about his relationship to her. If he hadn't been there, Randall wondered, would the younger man have made a play for Frankie?

Randall returned the look, wordlessly conveying a warning.

Billy immediately backed off. Turning back to the raised stage, he mumbled, "Anytime."

They handed out a few more cards, but Frankie was anxious to leave.

"We're going there tonight?" Randall asked as they made their way out of the establishment. "It's already after one. Don't you think that's a little late?"

"Not for an entertainer."

"But if he's sick—"

"Trust me, okay?"

"Why do you think he's faking it?"

"Because Marc doesn't particularly like to work. He's a great guitarist, Michael says. But he's always having to push him to make sure he shows up when he's supposed to. Things like that."

Suddenly, two men stepped out of the shadows a short distance from the door, accosting them as they walked down the sidewalk. One was tall and slimly built, the other shorter and much stubbier. It took only a second for Randall to recognize them as the men from the Cadillac.

"Well, well, well...look who's showed up," the taller man commented dryly. He seemed to appreciate his own attempt at threatening humor.

"Yeah," said his companion, "Mary and her little lamb." He reached out to tweak the point of Randall's collar. "Or maybe I should say *lambette.*" He laughed.

Randall had stiffened the instant he'd seen them. His first instinct was to pull Frankie behind him for protection, but she refused to budge. She stood at his side—stiff and straight and defiant. She was the first to reply, taunting, "Why don't you two go try out for a comedy club? There's bound to be one that isn't too picky."

"Nah," the taller man said, "we like doing what we're doing. It's got more... panache."

"Yeah... panache," his hatchet-faced partner echoed, grinning.

Frankie glanced at Randall and shook her head with pretended pity. "I doubt they even know what the word means."

The taller man took ahold of her arm and pulled her toward the shadows. When Randall reached out to stop him, he found his arms suddenly clamped from behind, and he, too, was propelled toward the darkness. The shorter man's strength was surprising. They were forced into an abbreviated alleyway. Frankie's mouth was muffled by a hand, her struggles restrained. Then both were shoved against some stacked milk crates, which caused several to fall. Randall tried to rush at their assailants, to do what he could to strike out against them, but a fist slammed into his stomach, doubling him over and making him gasp for breath.

"We got a message," the taller man, who seemed to be the leader of the two, said while trying to dodge Frankie's flailing feet. "Settle down," he threatened her, "or we'll make it harder for your little lamb."

Frankie ceased protesting.

The taller man smiled in satisfaction. "That's better," he said. "Now, listen, because I'm only going to say this once. We're running out of patience. Your brother has two days, Miss James. If the tape isn't back in the studio by then, we're going to make life hell for everyone who knows him. Starting with you! If you think this last week has been bad, just wait until Monday!''

"Go to hell!" Frankie spat out when her mouth was finally released.

The man turned to Randall. "And as for you—it took us a while to figure out who you were, but we finally did, Mr. Peters. My advice is you should mind your own business. We're not going to hurt your precious sister. We don't have any argument with her."

Randall drew as deep a breath as he could manage and wheezed, "Michael James is my client. That *makes* him my business."

The tall man tsked to his companion. "Now, that was a bad decision, wasn't it, Kenny? A very bad decision. It looks like maybe we should show you why." He nodded and Kenny slammed another fist into Randall's midsection.

Randall bent forward, clutching his stomach as pain exploded through his midsection. Kenny drew back for yet another blow, but Randall had no desire to be used as a punching bag. He forced himself to spring forward, knocking the man over with his surprise move. The two men struggled on the cement until finally, Randall ended up on top. That was when Kenny's partner decided to jump into the fray. He stepped closer to deliver a swift kick to Randall's ribs. But

Frankie didn't remain still. She rushed around the taller man and slung her purse in an arc that hit him squarely in the back of his knee. The knee buckled and since all his weight was balanced on it, the man went down in a heap, falling on his partner just as Randall rolled away.

Frankie helped Randall scramble to his feet. He squeezed her hand and off they ran.

As they neared the car, Frankie started to laugh. It was nervous laughter—high-pitched and high-strung. But it didn't prevent her from slinging open the door, jumping into the driver's seat and, once she was sure Randall was in the car, accelerating quickly into the street.

A ball of fire burned in Randall's stomach. He had no intention of joining in with her laughter, but giddiness over the physical danger they had just escaped soon had him laughing, as well.

Finally, Frankie was able to sober herself enough to ask, "Are you all right? They didn't damage anything seriously, did they?"

"Other than my pride, no," Randall said, still grinning widely.

"That man looked so surprised when you came at him. He never expected anything like that. And to tell you the truth, neither did I."

"I guess I just don't take kindly to being threatened."

"No," she said, and took a second away from driving to look at him. "Not by anyone, right?"

Obviously, she was referring to the time when *she* was the one doing the threatening. "Not by anyone," he agreed.

"Thanks for saying you're Michael's lawyer."

"That's what we agreed on, isn't it?"

"I still wasn't completely sure you meant it."

"I meant it."

She chanced another look, giving him a warmer smile than she had ever given him before. Then once again, she sobered. "This is only getting worse for Michael, isn't it? Oh, I wish none of it had ever happened! I wish Michael was back at Glass House working on his new album, and that I—" She stopped abruptly.

"That you what?" Randall asked, straightening slowly, attempting not to place too much stress on his battered stomach muscles. He had gathered other scrapes and bruises, but it was his midsection that hurt the most.

"That everything was back to normal. Peaceful and quiet."

"Somehow I can't see things ever being peaceful and quiet around you. You're one of those people 'things' seem to happen to."

"No, I'm not."

Randall snorted his disagreement.

"I'm not!" she claimed, insistent.

Randall looked out the window. He didn't have either the energy or the inclination to continue arguing, even if some of the fire was beginning to ease in his middle. As the streets flashed by, he realized that he found them unfamiliar. "Where are we going?" He frowned, puzzled.

"To see Marc."

"Still?" he asked, amazed.

"I don't see why not." So saying, she slowed the car and slipped into a parking space.

They were on a side street, away from the flow of traffic. The area was a mixed neighborhood of houses and converted warehouses. All signs pointed to everyone being asleep, except for a lighted window on the top story of one of the warehouses.

The three-story building was still being renovated. Inside, little looked complete. Doors were missing, sawhorses and building materials remained just as the workers had left them. But the elevator hummed with efficiency, and soon, they were on the top floor, where the doors swished open to reveal a gigantic room compartmentalized by movable screens.

Huge, white statues in various stages of dress and undress welcomed visitors with signs hung round their necks announcing: Living Room, Dining Room, Play Room, Kitchen.... Frankie blinked and glanced at Randall, who was having a hard time keeping a straight face. For some reason, the whimsical decor appealed to him.

"Hello, Marc?" Frankie called. She took a cautious step out of the elevator while Randall prevented the door from closing.

There was no reply. She tried again. "Marc, it's Frankie. Remember me? Michael's sister." A noise came from somewhere in the depths of the room. Frankie stopped, waiting.

A male figure staggered into the makeshift hall. Young and slim, he wore only low-slung jeans and the large tattoo of a flying dragon spread over his shoulder. His pale blond hair was long and disheveled, strands falling in front of his face, and dangling from his hand was a beer can. He peered at them, squinting, trying to focus.

"Frankie?" he slurred. "I don' remember no Frankie. No, wait—" He waved an aimless hand. "Oh, hey, I do! Frankie James! Mike's sister. What'cha doin' here, Frankie?"

Frankie moved quickly to the man's side and helped support him as he started to collide with one of the screens. A happy grin spread over the young man's face, his arm falling over her shoulders as he staggered against her, causing her to stagger. "Have you come to play with me, Frankie? My play room's messed up right now, but all we have to do is push everything to one side. The bed's all soft and cushy..." His lips managed to brush the side of her mouth. Frankie made a face at the potency of his breath, while Randall stepped forward, surprised by the rush of anger he felt at the fact that Frankie was so near to the drunken man.

Marc's head jerked up, went too far and lolled forward again before finally settling in some semblance of normalcy. "Hey!" he challenged. "Who are you?"

"A friend," Frankie explained as Randall took the younger man's other arm and relieved her of his weight. "Let's get him to the kitchen," she murmured, leading the way by following the signs.

The kitchen consisted of a minirefrigerator sitting on the floor, a hot plate, a rickety table and two chairs. The refrigerator was filled with beer cans and a half bottle of milk that had gone sour some days before.

"Do you have any coffee?" Frankie asked as Randall positioned his charge in a chair.

Marc motioned tipsily toward a cupboard against the wall.

Frankie came back with a partially filled jar of instant coffee and a small bag of sugar. At the freestanding sink, she filled a pot with water and put it on the hot plate to heat. Then she came back to sit in the remaining chair.

"It'll take more coffee than you have there," Randall said with disgust.

"Maybe not," she replied.

Marc's smile was beatific. He made an attempt to take Frankie's hand, missed, and tried again. He only succeeded in the end because she helped.

"Friends are so 'portant when a person's in trouble, don't you think?" he slurred.

"They certainly are," Frankie agreed.

"Like me," he continued. "I stick by my friends. And if I was in trouble, I'd expect my friends to stick by me."

The water had heated enough. Randall found a cup, washed it as best he could, ladled in several heaping teaspoons of coffee, poured in some water and placed it on the table.

"Drink it," Frankie encouraged.

"I'd rather have somethin' else, thanks," Marc said.

Frankie smiled. "Will you do it for me?" she asked.

A sloppy grin spread over Marc's good-looking features. "For you . . . anything!"

His aim was off on his first attempt, but he finally managed to grasp the cup and direct it to his mouth.

"It's hot!" he complained after his first sip.

"It's supposed to be," Frankie assured him.

Several cups later, Marc had to run for the bathroom. When he returned, he was white and shaken, but definitely more sober.

"Lord, that was awful. I *hate* coffee! I only keep it for guests." He fell back into his chair, exhausted, his skin looking clammy as he wiped at his lips with a trembling hand.

"Do you want something to eat?" Frankie asked. "Crackers? Pretzels? I saw some in the cupboard."

Marc refused quickly, as if afraid she might go get them. "Nothing, thanks."

Randall watched as the younger man rubbed his throbbing head, and he felt a spark of compassion. But his sympathy remained tempered by the resentment he still harbored for Marc's earlier behavior toward Frankie.

Frankie showed the compassion that Randall withheld. "I'm sorry to have to ask you this now, Marc. I know how you must feel. But I've heard that you've been in contact with Michael. That you've seen him. Is it true?"

Marc slowly lifted his head. "I saw him," he confirmed.

Frankie sat forward, unable to contain her excitement. "Where?" she demanded. "Was he all right?"

"It was just for a second or two," Marc said. "He was moving from one place to another. And, yeah, he looked okay."

"When was this?" Randall broke in.

Marc twisted to look at him. "Two days ago. Who *are* you anyway? What business is it of yours?"

"I'm Susan's brother. Was she with him?"

"No, at least, not at that moment. Someone was waiting for him, though. It could have been Susan. She was tall."

"What did he say?" Frankie asked urgently, unable to wait any longer.

"He just told me to be careful."

"Nothing else?"

"Well..." he said hesitantly, looking deeply into the imploring blue eyes, "he told me that the Masseys meant business. That he was really afraid something bad was going to happen.''

''Did he say anything about me? Did he ask you to give me a message?''

Marc shook his head. At her crestfallen expression, he said, ''It's not a good idea for you to get involved in this right now, Frankie. You don't know what you're up against.''

''I believe I do. I've met them.''

Marc gazed at her, gauging her mettle. ''And you're still determined,'' he stated slowly.

''He's my brother,'' she said simply.

Marc lifted bloodshot eyes to Randall. ''If you like her, keep her out of this, okay?''

''I can't *keep* her from anything. She does what she wants.''

The younger man smiled slightly. ''Just like Michael. They're two of a kind.''

''Do you think you'll see him again?'' Frankie demanded.

''I told you. I only met him by accident.''

Frankie didn't fully believe that. ''If you do,'' she said. ''Tell him I'm not going to stop looking for him until I find him. Tell him I've found a lawyer who's willing to help. Tell him it's Susan's brother. Tell him he *has* to contact us. Will you do that, Marc? Will you?''

Marc took the card and looked narrowly at Randall. "Sure," he said. "Why not? But I'm not making any promises. Things are a little rough right now."

"So you decided to obliterate your mind," Randall charged. "Smart move."

"Everybody has their own way of dealing with pressure."

"Well, next time, pick a better place to do it. If we can walk in on you, so can anyone else. That's not being very careful."

Marc shrugged. "Hey, when it's your time to go, man, you go. There's nothing you can do about it."

"You can take precautions."

"Depends upon the kind of life you want to lead. Me? I don't want to mess with all that garbage. If they want me, they can come get me."

Randall wondered how deeply the young man's bravado would go if he were faced with imminent danger. Would he just stand there and let someone attack? Randall seriously doubted it.

Frankie stood up, extending her hand. "Take care of yourself, Marc. Don't do anything silly."

Marc uncurled from his chair and, after running long fingers through his hair to brush disheveled strands away from his face, he accepted Frankie's hand. "I won't," he promised.

Frankie smiled and moved with Randall into the makeshift hallway. When they were almost at the elevator, Marc called after them, "The same goes for you, okay?"

Both were silent during the elevator ride downstairs. Once on the bottom floor, though, Randall asked, "Do you think he knows where Michael is?"

She shrugged. "He might, he might not."

"Why wouldn't he tell you if he did? Why would he hold back?"

"Out of a sense of loyalty? I don't know. All we can hope is that he'll get a message through to Michael to call us."

"But he told someone that he'd seen him. Isn't it dangerous for both of them that he's so loose lipped?"

"Maybe he didn't tell anyone."

"Then how—"

"People see things. Word gets around. That's what we've been trying to do. Get the word out and moving. *Our* word."

"How long have you known him?" Randall asked, remembering the younger man's attraction to Frankie.

"Who?" Frankie asked, unsure.

Randall jerked a thumb back toward the building they had just left. "Him."

"Awhile. Why?"

"Seems like he'd like to get to know you better."

She took his implication and didn't like it. "He was drunk! Anyway, Marc thinks every woman he meets wants to go to bed with him. A lot of band people think that way.''

"So—do you?''

Frankie whirled to face him, unwilling to have him question her any longer. "Exactly what business is that of yours? You're not my keeper. Nothing gives you the right to pry into my life!''

The smooth hum of a car's engine cut into the quietness of night. Startled, they both turned to see the black Cadillac run up close beside them. Tonight, the men seemed able to follow them at will.

"Trouble in paradise?'' the shorter man asked through the rolled down window. "Aw. Isn't that a shame? And to think, you were getting along so well just a little while ago, all kissy-kissy.''

They had even seen that! Frankie ran up to the Cadillac and kicked it, leaving a shallow dent in the passenger door.

Her action surprised everyone. "Hey!'' the stocky man cried. The Cadillac screeched to a stop.

Randall grabbed Frankie's hand and started to run. Their feet pounded the pavement. The Civic was parked just around the next corner. If they could make it before they were caught from behind . . .

The keys were in Frankie's hand. Randall grabbed them, unlocked the driver's door, jumped inside and somehow managed to start the car while unlocking the opposite door at the same time. Frankie was inside in a flash. "Do you know what you're doing?'' she asked, panting, while affixing her seat belt.

Randall didn't take time to answer. He slammed the car out of the parking space, screeching the tires and praying that, for once, the little car wouldn't falter. It didn't. But the Cadillac turned the corner right behind them and was soon on their tail. Frankie twisted around and saw them. A worried look flashed over her face. "I shouldn't have done that, should I?" she ventured.

"It didn't help," Randall bit out, taking a corner at speed. He gunned the car into the next block. The Cadillac followed.

She watched where they were going, an arm braced against the dashboard. "Turn right up there," she dictated. "Now!"

Randall did as she said. She seemed to know the city better than he did, even though he had lived there for years. "Now left!" she barked. The car swerved, tires screeched. "Now right again! All right...gun it! Get us over this hill, then take a right at the top. The first street." They practically flew up the hill. Then at the top, Randall slammed on the brakes, turned right and raced down the intersecting street.

"*Slow down!*" Frankie yelled.

His foot jerked off the accelerator.

"Turn right again," she said carefully, banking down her anxiety. "Slowly. Legally."

He did exactly as she said.

The men in the Cadillac, thinking they could catch up, roared around each corner, then down the street they were on.

Almost immediately, a set of flashing lights switched on and a siren blipped. A patrol car that had been lurking nearby caught up with the speeding Cadillac. Inside, a policeman motioned for the driver to pull over.

As Frankie watched through the rear window, a wide grin lighted her face. "Yes!" she cried in victory. "It worked!" Impulsively, she hugged Randall's arm. "We did it! *You* did it! You're a pretty good driver, you know that?"

Randall grinned in return. Never in his life had he gone through such an experience. And never in his life had he felt so alive! He asked, "Did you see that patrol car? Is that why you told me to slow down?"

She nodded, her grin increasing.

Still holding his arm, she looked something like a child at Christmas. A child who just knew that Santa was going to give her everything that she asked for. Randall wanted to hug her in return. He wanted to lift her high in the air and whirl her around until they were both dizzier than they were now!

"Make a U-turn at the corner," she directed, her eyes shining. "Let's go back and see what's happening."

"Do you think that's a good idea?" He was unsure.

"Sure. They're not going to go anywhere with that policeman writing them a ticket."

Once again, Randall did as Frankie said. And he had to admit that it felt good. As they rolled slowly by, the two men in the Cadillac looked at them, unable to do anything more than just stare. Frankie even waved, nudging Randall to join in. At the corner she settled back into her seat, chuckling. "Oh, that was *fine!*" she said approvingly. "Perfect! The look on their faces!"

Randall drove quickly out of the area. "Where to now?" he asked, realizing that he was not at all tired. The juices were truly flowing, and he couldn't have slept even if he'd tried.

"Back to your friend's place, I should think. We should be safe there for a little while longer. They know who you are now, but not where you are. And those two aren't going to follow us right away."

"There's no one else to see tonight?" Randall asked.

She glanced at <u>him</u>, sensing his regret. "Disappointed?" she teased.

"No..." Randall hedged. But strangely, he found that he was.

"We probably should call your answering service and see if we have any messages. It's been a while."

Randall nodded in agreement, but only a portion of his mind was attending to what she said. The rest was preoccupied with the ramifications of another, more basic question. What in the name of heaven was being with this woman starting to *do* to him?

Chapter Ten

Frankie stepped out of the shower refreshed, a smile on her lips, a song running through her mind. This was the best she had felt in ages. Two weeks to be exact. No, longer than that. She hadn't felt this good in . . . she didn't know when exactly.

Not even the knowledge that no one had tried to contact them through the evening had brought her spirits down. Someone would; she was positive. Probably tomorrow. Possibly even Michael himself. Marc would pass their message on to him, and he would call. All they had to do was wait.

They. She and Randall Peters.

Her confidence experienced a momentary bobble, but she quickly put it to rights. What had happened between them on the street by the club had been due to their unusual circumstance. She had been frightened and worried. Her defenses were down. It wouldn't happen again. Ever.

After dressing in a pair of comfortable jeans and the loose T-shirt she had taken to sleeping in over the past couple of weeks, she found her way down to the kitchen. She hadn't felt like dressing up again. Her hair was left to its usual short feathering around her face, and she hadn't bothered to add makeup. After all, it was three o'clock in the morning! The only reason they were still up was hunger. Breakfast had been a long time ago.

Randall, too, had gotten more comfortable, stripping down to the pair of black pants and a short, paisley robe he must have found in his friend's closet. As with everything else his friend owned, the robe showed good taste. It was dark blue, with splashes of lighter blue, red, green and gold forming the centuries-old pattern. It probably looked good on his friend, but it looked just as good on Randall.

Randall turned from investigating the contents of the refrigerator when he heard her come into the room. He started to speak, but the words remained unsaid, his eyes widening as he took in her fresh appearance.

"Find anything?" she asked, uncomfortable being the object of his appraisal.

"Not a lot," he said. "They must have emptied it of almost everything before they left. There's margarine, a few eggs, some onions."

"Cheese?" she asked.

He checked. "Yes."

"Then how about an omelet?"

"Sounds great. Am I the cook, or are you?"

"Do you cook?" she asked, leaning against the island work space.

"I make the best Pasta Primavera in town."

She smiled slightly. "That's good, then. Cook away. I'm not very talented in that direction."

"You don't like to cook?"

"I didn't say that. I just don't do it very well."

"That's probably because no one ever took the time to teach you."

"How did you learn?" she asked, curious. Michael was a total incompetent in a kitchen, and her grandfather thought that cooking was women's work.

"Well, on my own, with the help of a few good cookbooks. But it came about from necessity. I got tired of eating in restaurants all the time."

"What a hard life," she said dryly.

"It gets boring."

He removed the eggs from the refrigerator and placed them on the counter. Then he set to work chopping the slender green onions into tiny bits. "Put a pat of margarine into the smaller skillet, will you?" he directed. "That is, if you'd like to help." He had already found and laid out two skillets. "Okay, now sauté these, just get them soft." He swept chopped bits of onion into the melted margarine.

"I know what *sauté* means," she snipped.

He handed her a spatula, grinning.

She stirred while the eggs were broken and whipped.

"About done?" he asked a few minutes later.

She nodded.

He adjusted the flame beneath the second skillet, waited for it to heat, then added a bit of margarine and a small amount of peanut oil he had found in the cupboard. Once that, too, was heated, he poured in the egg mixture and carefully spread it around by swirling the skillet.

Francesca watched, fascinated, as he loosened the sides of cooking egg and allowed the uncooked portion to slip beneath. He repeated the process several times as the egg cooked.

"Okay, now the onions." He waited for her to sprinkle them on. "Only on one half," he instructed.

"What about the cheese?" she asked.

"That comes in a minute."

He located a dinner plate, slid part of the omelet onto the surface, then expertly folded the remaining half onto the base.

The processed cheese was presliced. He cut two pieces in half, arranged the triangles on top of the hot omelet and watched as they melted, perfectly in place.

"Voilà!" he cried proudly, extending the plate for her inspection.

"Very nice," she said, her stomach rumbling.

He cut the concoction in half and slid a portion onto another plate.

"That's it, I'm afraid. There's no bread."

"This is fine," Francesca murmured, already slipping into a chair.

Randall found forks in a drawer and handed one to her as he took a chair of his own. After a bite, he sounded his approval. "Umm."

She flashed a smile, seconding that opinion.

The tea kettle whistled and Randall got up. A moment later, he came back with both tea bags and instant coffee. Francesca chose a tea bag.

No further words were exchanged as they concentrated on their meager meal. But in the end, Francesca sat back, satisfied. "That was delicious," she said. "The best omelet I've ever tasted."

"You were hungry."

She returned his smile. "Well, that, too." Then she couldn't prevent a yawn.

"And tired," he said, laughing.

He had a nice laugh, she decided. Then she wiped the thought from her mind. "Aren't you?" she asked.

"I was. Now—" He shrugged. He played with the handle of his coffee cup, his gaze fixed on nothing in particular, giving her an opportunity to study him.

His light brown hair accented his coloring perfectly, curling slightly, looking bright and alive. His skin was either naturally tan or he had spent some time in the sun. His straight nose was neither too wide nor too narrow, and his glasses didn't detract from his eyes, which were rimmed with dark lashes. His cheekbones were nicely curved, jaw and chin adequately strong. His mouth.... Francesca's gaze skittered away, her attention then centering on his ringless left hand. She fidgeted in her chair.

Randall looked up, his gray eyes curious. "Do you want to go to bed? If you do, go ahead. I'll clean up."

Francesca had jumped at the unexpectedness of his first question and spent the remainder of the time he spoke acting as if she hadn't. "No, I'll help," she felt compelled to say.

Neither made a move to get up. Francesca took a sip of her tea only to find that it had cooled.

"You want more of that?" he asked.

She nodded.

He put water on to boil and sat back down, again fingering the handle of his cup.

Outside, the night was especially quiet, as if a heavy fog had rolled in to mute all sound.

"Tell me about Michael," Randall said at last. "If I'm going to help him, I should know something about him."

She looked up defensively. "What else do you need to know? I thought I'd already told you—"

"I mean about him personally," Randall said, interrupting. "How old is he? How long has he been making a living as a musician?"

"He's twenty-four. About three years. Before that, he worked as a carpenter."

"Building houses?"

"More like general construction. If someone needed a room added or some cabinets made, Michael could do it."

"Did he have a partner?"

"Off and on."

"What about his childhood? Where was he born? Where did he grow up?"

"I don't see where that—"

"It's something I'd like to know."

The teakettle whistled again and Randall got up to refill their cups. When he reseated himself across from her, Francesca said, "He was born in Salt Lake City."

"You, too?"

"No, Denver."

"Your father was transferred?"

She frowned. "We moved around a lot. He worked in construction."

"So you didn't really have any one place to call home."

"I still don't see where that—"

"Are your parents still alive?"

"Our mother is."

"Where does she live?"

"Outside Sacramento."

"Does she work?"

"She takes care of my grandfather."

He was quick to sense the strain that had entered her words. "You don't like him?"

She didn't want to talk about it. Particularly not to him. She pushed her chair away from the table. "Sometimes I forget you're a lawyer. Then you do something to remind me!"

He caught her hand to keep her from getting up. "Not all of us are the next best thing to thieves. Sometimes, we come in quite handy."

She tried to sustain her anger, but in the face of his steady gaze, she conceded that what he'd said was true.

She pulled her hand away. For the moment, they had traded places. He was the person in control now, she the one on slippery ground.

He smiled, a nice smile that didn't tout his advantage. "You and your grandfather didn't get along?" he asked quietly.

"No," she answered.

"What does your grandfather do for a living?"

"He's a farmer. He grows almonds. Acres and acres of almond trees."

"How did you come to live with him?"

Randall watched her squirm under his questioning. He didn't want to keep pressing, but he knew that if he didn't, she would tell him nothing. And he needed to know more. About her brother. About her.

When she had walked into the room earlier, wearing a pair of washed out jeans and that baggy T-shirt, all signs of makeup scrubbed away and smelling freshly of soap and shampoo, he had been shocked. She claimed to be twenty-six, but she looked so much younger. At the same time, she was even more beautiful than he remembered. Her skin was clear and glowing, her hair was left to fall freely against her face. Like a chameleon, she kept changing right in front of his eyes, and he wondered, inexplicably, if one day, she would just disappear from his life as suddenly as she had appeared in it. He *had* to know more about her!

She explained stiffly, "Our father died when I was twelve and Michael was ten. Our mother wasn't trained for any kind of job, and our grandfather offered us a roof. It was... difficult. Our grandfather never let her forget that our father died without leaving us enough money to get by on. He considered Dad a failure and her, too, because she hadn't listened to him when he'd ordered her not to marry our father." Francesca looked up with an expression of defiance and pain. "Is that the kind of thing you want to know?"

Randall returned her gaze, not trying to hide his compassion. He nodded.

Like flood waters bursting through an earthen dam, the words came quickly, urgently. "He hated the idea that Michael loved music. He did everything he could to break him of it. He destroyed every record and tape that Michael owned. He gave away our radio. He even smashed the guitar our father gave Michael just a few days before he died, the one that his dad had learned to play on when he was a boy. Grandfather didn't let Michael visit any of his friends because he said they were a bad influence. He made him work until he dropped from exhaustion." Her hands were curled into fists on the edge of the table, the knuckles showing white.

"Was he just as hard on you?" Randall asked. He wanted to reach out to her, to soothe her, to make up for what had happened in the past, but he knew that she would reject such an intrusion. All he could do was let her talk.

"Girls don't count, in his opinion," she said bitterly. "I was there to keep the house clean. That's all."

"Did he object to you having friends?"

"I didn't let him stop me," she flared. "Michael tried not to, either, but it was harder for him."

Randall could see where the seeds of her defiance had been born. "What about your mother? Couldn't she have found someplace else to live? It doesn't take a lot of education to get a simple job."

Something in the woman sitting so tautly across from him became even tauter. "My mother did the best she could." Her voice was level, the words practiced, as if she had told herself that more than once throughout her childhood and beyond.

"And she still lives with him?" he asked quietly, still probing.

"Yes."

"Do you visit her?"

"She visits me. I won't see that man anymore. Not after what he did to Michael."

"But Michael's a success now, in music."

"I'm not talking about that! Inside—he hurt Michael inside."

And he had hurt her, as well, Randall surmised. Her mother had, too. Witnessing her mother's weakness in the face of her grandfather's abuse must have been terribly difficult for someone as fiercely independent as Frankie. Maybe that was why she was so determined to be strong, to be tough, to meet problems head-on and try to enact a solution, even if the odds were stacked against her. "And what have you done with your life?" he asked softly. "You don't like to cook. That's about all I know about you except that you've held down an interesting variety of short-term jobs."

"There isn't anything else," she said.

"What about a job now? Have you settled into something, or are you still jumping from place to place?"

Frankie stood up. "That's enough. I don't want to talk about it anymore. The meal was nice. Thank you. Now, if you don't mind—"

Randall's gaze was quietly assessing. It was obvious that she thought she had told him too much, which only underlined another detail he knew about her: she was an intensely private person. "Thank you, too," he said. "What you've told me will go no farther."

The china blue eyes flickered over him, then she left.

For a long while, Randall continued to sit at the table, thinking about everything he had learned.

THE INSISTENT RING of a telephone broke into Randall's sleep. He had no idea what time it was or what day it was, his slumber had been so deep. But the familiar voice of his secretary soon had him sitting up. That and the information she imparted.

"I'm sorry to call you so early, Mr. Peters," she said. "But the answering service has been trying to get you. It's an urgent message from someone named... Anne? Or it could be Annie? I think you'll want to hear it."

Randall rubbed the vestiges of sleep from his face and blinked at the bedside clock. The hands read seven-thirty. He'd only been asleep about two hours. "What is it?" he asked.

"She said she thinks she's remembered something. She wants to meet with you this morning, but she doesn't want you to come to her apartment. Something about her husband not being happy if he knew what she was doing. Does that mean anything to you?"

It did, and it didn't surprise him. "Where does she want to meet?"

"She said for you to park as closely as you can to the Conservatory of Flowers in Golden Gate Park and that you can meet her outside the front doors at nine o'clock. She said not to be late."

Randall checked the clock again and pushed away from the bed. "Thanks," he said. "We'll be there."

He hung up the phone and dressed as quickly as he could in another of the shirt-and-jeans combinations that Frankie had picked out for him. In this one, the jeans were normal, except for the chains stretched across the crotch. They matched the chains on the biker boots, he thought wryly, as well as the metal studs that were hammered into the thick denim of the accompanying jacket. It was a look not to be believed by anyone who knew him. But he had to admit, he didn't feel nearly as strange as he had that first day. He was even beginning to have fun with it. Randall paused, his hand on the doorknob. *He was beginning to have fun with it?*

He tapped on the door a short distance down the hall. He had to tap again before he received an answer. The voice sounded muffled, aroused too soon from sleep.

"We've had a message," he called through the door.

A second later, the door opened. Her face retained the freshness of the night before. Her blond hair was still feathered around her face, mussed somewhat but too short to be tangled. The loose T-shirt showed a length of nicely turned leg. She looked all soft and warm and appealing, and Randall couldn't help his masculine response.

"What is it?" she asked, breathless from her race across the room.

"A message from Anne LeBaron. She wants to meet us at nine o'clock. She's remembered something."

Frankie's disappointment was hard to disguise, but she quickly brightened. "At least that's something. What time...?" She frowned, having forgotten.

"We'll have to leave in an hour."

"All right. I'll be down."

She started to close the door, but Randall stopped her. It wasn't that he had something important to say. He just didn't want to be closed away from her softness, her warmth. "Would you like a roll or something for breakfast? There's a bakery down the street. I can go get something while you dress."

She started to refuse, then thought better of it. "That's probably a good idea. Especially after yesterday."

"Are you insulting my omelet?" he teased.

The dimple appeared when she smiled. "I was thinking of the length of time between meals. You seem to get testy when you're hungry."

"I like it when you do that," he murmured, his eyes moving from the slight indentation to wander over the rest of her face.

"Do what?" she asked, the dimple disappearing, her body tensing warily.

"Smile," he said simply.

Her eyes intensified in color for a second before becoming hooded. "I'll be down in a few minutes," she said levelly and closed the door.

RANDALL WALKED with a spring to his step as he made his way to the bakery. He didn't care that he received odd looks from some of the upscale people walking in the neighborhood. Blond hair, a beautiful face and china blue eyes were all too prominent in his mind.

When he returned to Paul's house, he found Frankie waiting in the kitchen. She was dressed conservatively in jeans and a white, buttoned shirt over which she had pulled a dark blue sweater. He flashed a quick smile as she looked up at him.

Coffee had just finished dripping in the machine, its aroma tantalizing to the senses.

"I hope you like croissants," he said.

"I love them," she said, her enthusiasm slightly stiff, as if in the time it had taken her to get dressed and him to go to the bakery, she had remembered all that she told him in the early hours of the morning and was still of two minds as to whether or not she had done the right thing.

He opened the bag and held it out to her. "Fresh from the oven. The lady told me she'd just baked them. They're still warm."

Frankie made a selection and settled in a chair. Randall claimed the opposite chair and glanced at his watch. They still had half an hour to kill.

"They're good," he pronounced after taking a bite.

"Mmm," she replied, having followed suit.

They munched in silence for several minutes. Both croissants were soon devoured.

"Want another?" he asked.

Frankie shook her head. After a moment, she asked, "I wonder what Anne remembered?"

Randall shrugged. He looked at his watch again. Twenty minutes. They needed something to help pass the time. "Do you play gin?" he asked suddenly.

She looked at him as if he had proposed something shocking. "What?"

"Gin rummy. The card game. If you do, we can—"

"No." She shook her head.

"Want to learn?"

"No."

He sighed.

"I'm not very good at games," she explained, relenting from her hard position. "My attention wanders."

"You sound like Susan. I never could teach her the game—any game, really. I always had to tell her when it was her turn, and that takes half the fun out of it. She was like that from the time she was a little girl."

Francesca studied him. "There's quite a difference between your ages, isn't there? I know Susan turned twenty-one last spring. And you're . . . ?"

He laughed. "I'm an old man with one foot in the grave."

"I didn't say that."

"I'm thirty-six."

"Susan told me you practically raised her."

"She must have said a lot that one time she talked about me," he reminded, giving her a look of teasing estimation.

"Well," Frankie admitted, "it might have been more than once."

Just as he'd suspected. She had used the idea of Susan's seeming reticence as a weapon against him when they'd first met.

"What else did she say?" he asked.

Francesca shrugged uncomfortably. She knew she had finally been caught out. "Not a lot."

Randall let her off the hook. He sat back in his chair and watched her face as he explained, "Our parents died in a car crash when Susan was thirteen. I did the best I could for her, but an aunt of ours thought it would be better for Susan to live with her. A woman's influence and all that. Susan wasn't happy, so she spent most of her time with me, which didn't please our aunt. But there wasn't much of anything she could do about it."

"Did she make Susan's life miserable?" Frankie asked, thinking of her own life.

"No, mostly mine. She kept telling me I was a bad influence."

Frankie's eyes widened. "You?"

"My aunt thought I should get married, and I didn't oblige her."

"You've never been married?"

"No." Then he asked quickly, "Have you?"

She blinked at his dexterity. "No."

"Good." He smiled and, a moment later, re-checked his watch. "We can leave now," he said. "A few minutes to spare won't hurt."

Frankie stood up. One word seemed to echo in the room around them, his satisfactorily expressed, *good*.

Chapter Eleven

Anne LeBaron wasn't at the designated meeting spot when Frankie and Randall arrived, but they were early, so they didn't worry about it. When fifteen minutes elapsed and she still hadn't shown up, they began to grow concerned.

"What do you think happened?" Frankie asked, her brow knitting. "Do you think Monk—"

"Let's hope not. Maybe she just got caught in traffic or her bus broke down."

"I don't like this," Frankie began, "something doesn't—" Her words broke off.

Randall swung round to see what she was looking at.

Monk LeBaron was coming up the walkway, his bearing similar to that of a bulldozer plowing up trees. When he spotted them, his irritation only increased.

"I thought it'd be you two," he grumbled even before reaching them. "Can't leave well enough alone, can you? Got to push, get people in trouble." He stopped directly across from them.

"We don't want to get anyone in trouble, Monk," Randall said. He gauged the man's physical ability. Monk might look out of shape, but there was still a great deal of power remaining in his stocky body.

"Where's Anne?" Frankie asked, as usual not hesitating to thrust herself into the fray.

"She's at home where she should be, makin' my breakfast."

"Nursing a black eye?" Frankie challenged.

Monk rounded on her, causing Randall to warn, "Don't even think about it." This was said quietly but with enough force to make the man hesitate.

Monk flexed his shoulders, reasserting what he considered his authority. "I didn't come here to fight," he claimed. "I came to tell you to leave my wife alone! Don't try to see her again. Don't even try to talk to her. I don't want her having nothin' to do with you. I protect what's mine. Do you understand?"

"Sure. Yeah. We understand." Randall's contempt for the man was hard to mask, but he did sympathize with Monk's desire to shield his family. He felt the same way himself.

"Well, you'd better," Monk stressed. "If you know what's good for you."

"Just don't hurt her," Frankie argued. "She was only trying to help us."

"She helps too many damn people," Monk complained. "Too many!" he repeated before he turned to walk away.

The tension in the air drained as Monk's angry back disappeared from view.

Frankie looked at Randall. "Now what do we do?" she asked, not really expecting an answer.

"I don't know," Randall said, fully knowing that she didn't expect one.

"I think we should call Anne before Monk gets home, to see if she's all right."

"He'll probably be home before we can find a phone. They don't live that far away." He looked at the locked doors of the Conservatory behind them. The building wasn't open to the public yet, and he doubted that they could find anyone, even if someone were there.

Frankie grimaced in frustration. "I wonder what she wanted to tell us!"

Randall shook his head. "If it's important, she'll find a way of getting word to us. She did this morning."

"But Monk found out."

"She'll figure something out."

Frankie spun around, presenting her back to him.

Randall looked at the blond-capped head and the tiny body that held such a fiercely loyal heart. Sometimes he forgot how small she was, her personality held such force.

He stepped closer. "Everything will work out. I truly doubt the Masseys want to kill Michael. They just want to frighten him. Make him miserable. That's all."

"You don't know them," she said tightly.

"No, I don't," he agreed. "But I've known people very much like them. I've even worked for a few." He was silent. He hesitated to touch her, unsure of how she would react, but he found that he couldn't prevent himself. His fingers spread over her shoulders, feeling the substance of skin and bone. She stiffened at first, then allowed his touch. He did nothing to increase their intimacy. For the moment, offering comfort was enough.

The walk back to the car was subdued. They had started the morning with such high hopes. Of her own accord, Frankie went to the passenger door and started to slip inside, only to draw back in surprise. Randall, observing her reaction from the other side of the car, frowned in puzzlement. His frown deepened when she quickly bent to retrieve something from the passenger footwell. At her whoop of excitement, Randall jerked his own door open to meet her glowing face across the space of the seats.

"Randall! Look!" In her hands was a round container about a foot in diameter and an inch thick. He didn't understand. "It's the master!" she cried, being careful to keep the words muted. "Michael's master tape," she explained when he continued to look at her blankly.

Understanding finally dawned. For a moment, Randall felt excitement, too, then reality intervened. "How did it get here?" he asked. "Who would—"

Francesca jumped into the car and slammed the door shut, securing the door lock in almost the same second. "Hurry up," she cried. "Get inside! I haven't seen our shadows today, but that doesn't mean they aren't here. Get in, Randall. Get in!"

Randall jerked into action. He fell into his contoured seat and locked the door. "I still don't understand," he complained.

She turned a beaming face. "This meeting was a setup, don't you see? It was just an excuse to get us here, so the tape could be delivered. Anne must have been in on it. That's why it didn't matter whether she came or not. Or that Monk came, instead. Actually, if anyone was watching us, they were glued to what we were doing with him. Not to the car."

"And that's when someone put—"

"Correct!"

Randall looked at the box his companion was hugging so tightly. "Now what do we do?" he asked. And this time an answer was expected.

Francesca searched the area of the footwell and even the seat where she was sitting. "I thought there'd be a note," she murmured.

"Maybe it's inside."

She held the box away from her, stared at it for several seconds, then balancing it on her lap, undid the latch and lifted the cover off. On top of the reel was a folded square of paper. Francesca pounced on it. "It's from Michael," she said breathlessly, intent on following the hasty scrawl of words. "He says he's sending this to you. That Susan said you'd know what to do with it to keep it safe. He says they're all right and for us not to worry."

Randall's first reaction was surprise that Michael would turn such a precious commodity over to him, even on Susan's word. Then his surprise turned to anger, both for what Michael James had done, and for telling them not to *worry!* After everything they had been through?

Francesca was quick to sense the shift in Randall's emotions. "What is it? What's wrong? At least we've heard from them!"

"Somehow, that doesn't seem enough," Randall grated tightly.

She blinked. "Well, I think it is, for now. Without the tape, they're in less danger."

"And you're in a hell of a lot more!" he burst out. "You're not about to let me go off with it alone, are you? Your brother should have thought before he acted. He should have known! But that doesn't seem to be a strong point with him, does it? First, he steals the tape, then he takes the heat off himself by putting it onto you! Good God, what arrogance . . . or stupidity . . . or possibly both!"

"My brother isn't arrogant or stupid," she answered heatedly. "He's doing the best he can in a difficult situation."

"And putting a hell of a lot of people at risk while he's at it! If it was just him, it would be different! But he's involved you . . . and Susan."

"Susan came back from France voluntarily! He didn't ask her to!"

"Susan's just a kid. And I'll be the first to admit that she does stupid things sometimes!"

"Like falling in love with my brother?"

"Like falling in love with your brother!"

Frankie lapsed into silence, her face turned determinedly away from him. A moment later, she said icily, "I'm not going to discuss this with you right now. We have one priority. Whether you agree with it or not, we have to safeguard this tape. Susan said you'd know what to do with it."

Frustration mounted within Randall. He hadn't meant to come down on her so hard. This situation wasn't her fault. Just as it wasn't his. How could her brother so cavalierly deposit the tape with them and place her in such danger? She was loyal to him, but he wasn't loyal to her! Randall felt he was at least entitled to vent his displeasure. He swiveled to start the engine. "I don't know what to do with it!" he growled.

"Do you have a safety deposit box?" she asked.

He didn't answer.

She repeated, "I asked if you have a safety deposit box."

Randall jerked the car into gear and drove out of the parking place. "Not one big enough for that. But I do have something else."

"What?" she asked. "What is it?"

Again he didn't answer, which caused her to angrily twitch away from him. The journey continued in thick silence.

RANDALL WAS REQUIRED to show his credentials to the guard inside the building, then sign in before they could proceed to his office on the tenth floor. Because it was early Saturday morning, very few people were working. He led the way into the suite of rooms that made up the law firm's office. The decor was subtly tasteful, the carpet thick and the watercolors signed. Francesca didn't make a sound.

"Over here," he said, directing her into his personal office. The desk was made of dark mahogany, its surface clear except for a picture of Susan, and a pen set. A matching conference table was positioned a short distance away, and behind it was a wall lined with numerous sets of similarly bound books.

He walked to the far wall, where at the side of a narrow credenza, he bent to open his safe. "This is the best place I can think to put it. As you saw, the building is guarded day and night, both weekdays and weekends. It's wired. It's locked. And my secretary and I are the only two people who have this combination. Any more secure and you're in Fort Knox." The heavy door swung open. He looked up at her and extended his hand.

Francesca held the master tape protectively close to her breast. She met his clear, gray gaze, the gaze that merited the trust of numerous clients, and hesitated only a moment before yielding the tape into his care. Randall slipped it inside the safe, closed the door and gave the dial a final spin. "There," he said, straightening. "That's done."

"Yes," she agreed. Then she turned tightly and walked to the door, her back stiff, her manner distant.

Randall looked after her, puzzled. "Frankie? What are you doing?"

She spun around, her blue eyes flashing. "I'm leaving you alone. Isn't that what you want? You made yourself perfectly clear earlier. You don't like me. You don't like my brother. You don't like the situation we've put you in. I'm sorry you still have to watch out for the tape, but you're absolved of everything else. When I meet with the Masseys, I'll tell them you didn't have anything to do with this. That none of it was your idea. That should make you pretty safe."

Her words shocked him. He hadn't meant for her to take what he'd said that way. He was concerned for her, not for himself. But of all things, his mind centered on one idea. "Meet with the Masseys," he echoed hollowly.

"Sure. Why not?" she challenged.

"Because it's crazy, that's why!"

She opened the door, refusing to listen. "Someone has to talk with them and get this all straightened out. Why not me?"

Randall stared at her. "Larceny doesn't run in your family. *Lunacy* does!"

"It's been nice meeting you, too." Her mocking tone reminded him of the early hours of their acquaintance. Then she started to step outside.

"Frankie!" he called, lunging for the door, but she was quick and had already closed it behind her. He fumbled with the doorknob before finally releasing it, and was in time to see her run out of the suite toward the elevator. As luck would have it, the car had not left the floor and when she pressed the call button, the doors instantly swished open to allow her inside.

Randall picked up speed, trying to catch up, but the doors shut before he could get to them. He punched the call buttons for the remaining elevators, but none of the cars were there. In all likelihood, they were all nesting on the main floor. With growing impatience, he waited. Then he bolted for the stairwell, fully aware that once he started down, he would have no way out until he was on the main floor. That was another feature of the building's security. Still, running would be faster than waiting for an elevator to arrive. Randall lost count of floors during his dizzying descent. If it hadn't been for the cordoned off section of stairway leading to the building's basement, he would have accidentally gone farther.

Nearly out of breath, he burst through the stairwell door and was in time to see Francesca walking sedately across the lobby so as not to attract the guard's suspicion. He tried to yell, but the sound came out so weakly that no one farther away than the elevator bank could have heard him. He drew as deep a breath as he could and tried again. "Hey!" he yelled, this time successfully.

Francesca sped up to the door and pushed outside.

Randall ran after her, limping slightly, having banged his knee on one of the stair rails.

The guard hurried over to him. "Is there a problem, Mr. Peters?" he asked, his expression concerned. "Did the lady forget something?"

Randall shook off the guard's concern and hobbled through the door, feeling the man's puzzled gaze follow him. Then he saw that Francesca was running toward his car, which they had parked in the building's delivery zone. When she saw that he was not far behind, she hurriedly jumped inside and started the engine. Obviously she'd taken his keys from the top of his desk where he had put them earlier.

"Frankie!" Randall called, feeling his sense of impotence grow as she started to back into the street. "Frankie, wait!" he called again.

She didn't pause. As quickly as she could, she rammed the Civic into first gear and burst into the flow of traffic, instantly making her way into the far lane. When she passed him, they were separated by two rows of traffic.

Randall stood on the curbside, trembling. He was angry; he was frustrated. He would have strangled her himself if she hadn't been so far away. She had stolen his car! This after announcing that she was going to do something else he thought was about the silliest thing she could do next to teasing an enraged grizzly!

Randall started to pace up and down a short section of sidewalk. He didn't care who might be watching him. He didn't care if the guard might wonder at his sanity. He grumbled to himself, spitting out words, allowing his anger some release. But none of it did any good. Not even the, *"Fine! And I hope I never see you again, either!"* that he shouted to the back of his fast disappearing car.

RANDALL CONTINUED TO LIMP as he made his way to his apartment on Russian Hill. He had no reason to go back to Paul's except to clean the place up, and he would do that later. Right now, he couldn't face it.

The elevator to the third floor of his building hummed quietly, and Randall, in a surly mood, glowered. Yet he knew he should be happy! This was what he had been waiting for all along—to return to his apartment, to the peace and quiet of his domain where no airport personnel or crazy, blond dingbats could harass him. But he wasn't happy. Not in the tiniest bit, and he knew exactly who to blame.

The elevator doors slid open and he stepped into the hall, stopping at the entry door with the familiar bronze number. If he closed his eyes, would he be able to force a return to the serenity he had once found there? Would he be able to sit in his favorite chair, a favored CD on the player and a small glass of wine at his elbow as he reread a beloved book? He tried to envision it. Yes! But in his vision, a tiny frown soon darkened his brow and a concerned look clouded his eyes as they drifted repeatedly from the page... when he found himself worrying about what had become of *her!*

Randall jammed the key into the lock, pausing only to glance at the note someone from the cab company had left in the crack. It told him that he had one week in which to reclaim his garment bag. After smashing the note into a tight ball, he gave the key a savage twist. He didn't care *what* became of her. If she wanted to fight the Masseys alone, let her! If she was that determined... she had caused him nothing but trouble the entire time he had known her. But in the amount of time it took for him to reach the light switch, he knew that he didn't mean it. The problem was that he *did* care.

When he switched on the lights, Randall's thoughts drew to an abrupt halt. His apartment was a wreck! Everything lay in shambles! Books were tumbled from bookshelves, keepsakes were scattered on the carpet and his CD and vinyl record collections were tossed about with little care. Cushions were thrown off the couch, drapes were half off the wall and pictures were cockeyed on their hangers, if they remained on the wall at all. Drawers were emptied haphazardly.

He might have ascribed the damage to an earthquake if he hadn't known immediately who was at fault. Whoever had done this had been looking for something. And there was only one group of people he knew who were looking for something, the Massey brothers. Randall's jaw tightened as he continued to survey the damage. "Something else to thank her for!" he muttered. Then with spirits drooping, he walked slowly into the room, shook out a sofa cushion and settled it back in place so that he could sit down.

That was where Paul found him a half hour later, sitting motionless and staring into space. "Holy—" his friend said from the doorway as he took in the devastation. "Randall?"

Randall's gray eyes lifted. He was no longer surprised by anything. "You're back," he said.

Just as tall as Randall, but with dark hair and dark eyes, Paul Sullivan's leanly sculpted features reflected his shock. He said as if dazed, "We decided to come back early. Allison's feeling better now, and she wanted to be back in town for the opening night of Frank Alexander's play.... Randall! What happened?" Then his eyes widened even more as he noted his friend's unusual choice of clothing, from the chains across the crotch of his jeans to the metal-studded jacket. This was not something the Randall he knew would choose to wear.

"Is Allison with you?" Randall asked.

"No, she's back at our place. That's why I'm here. To check—Randall, did you use it yourself or did someone break in? There were dishes in the sink and our bed was disturbed, not to mention that a woman's suitcase was in the guest room."

"I borrowed some of your clothes, too," Randall confessed.

"*Those* aren't my clothes!" Paul was quick to deny.

Randall's face slowly cracked into a grin. Then he started to laugh, and for a moment, the laughter got away from him, just as it had a few days before when he had been pushed too far. He struggled to regain control. "I doubt you'd believe me, even if I told you what's happened," he said with a groan.

Paul repositioned a second cushion on the couch and sat down. "Try me," he said.

Randall buried his face in his hands and, after rubbing the skin roughly, straightened. "I'm sorry I left your place in such a mess. I was coming back to straighten it, but—"

"No problem. Now, what's happened? You look ... different. And it's not just the clothes. It's— Who's the woman, Randall? Is she the reason you—"

Randall exploded, "She's a pigheaded, stubborn, crazy, insane— If I don't *ever* see her again, I'll be a happy man!"

Some of Paul's concern faded into a smile. "So, you like her. Who is she?"

Randall shook his head. "I don't know *what* I feel for her. Right now, I'd gladly—"

Paul's smile increased. "Sounds like love to me."

"Well, it's not!"

His friend shrugged at Randall's hot denial.

"She's someone I agreed to help," Randall explained. "Someone Susan knows." It was too much, at the moment, to explain Susan's relationship with

Frankie's brother, something he heartily wished would just dissolve so he would never have to explain anything to anyone.

"What sort of trouble is she in?" Paul asked.

"Some people are threatening her brother. Some people who like to play rough. I've agreed to represent him, so to speak."

"And that's why—" Paul indicated the room.

"Yep."

"Any why you're—" He motioned to Randall's clothes.

"Yep."

"Isn't this a little out of your line?"

"I didn't ask for it!" Randall proclaimed, again giving vent to anger and frustration. "She forced me!" Then when he realized how stupid that sounded, he quickly backtracked. "She put it to me in such a way that I couldn't refuse. Susan's involved. If I don't help, she could get hurt."

"Have you reported this to the police?"

"We can't! Don't ask. It's all so damned complicated." Randall stood up, no longer able to remain still.

Paul watched him pace, his dark eyes contemplative. "Do you need any help?" he asked at last.

Randall stopped to look at his friend. They were as close as two men could be, nearly brothers. Since their college days, they had helped each other repeatedly. They'd watched as each struggled to make it in their respective fields and had watched as each made mistakes in business and in their personal lives. They'd been there when all that was needed was something as simple as a friendly word. Randall shook his head. "I don't want you involved in this. I can handle it."

Paul glanced around the room again. "You want some help cleaning this up?"

Randall again shook his head.

Paul stood. He put a hand on his friend's shoulder and gave it a firm shake. "Just watch out for yourself. Don't do anything stupid. And if you change your mind or decide that I can be of some use, just give me a call."

"I will," Randall said.

Paul's hand fell away and a slow smile touched his lips. "Are we ever going to meet this lady? She must be something if she can get you so worked up. When everything's over and done with, bring her by."

"You don't know what you're asking!" Randall warned.

The smile grew. "Makes me want to meet her all the more."

Once Paul had left the apartment, Randall returned to the couch. A visit from his best friend should have steadied him, but it hadn't. In fact, it had had the reverse effect. Randall didn't love Frankie. He couldn't! She was the exact opposite of everything he had always strived for. He wanted a calm center and predictable outcomes. Things *happened* when she was around. When she came into a room, even the molecules in the air started to dance. And as far as predictability went, she was the complete antithesis! He *never* knew what she'd do next!

He didn't love her. He couldn't! Could he?

Chapter Twelve

Randall slept in his own bed that night for the first time in nearly a week. At least, he tried to sleep. It felt more like he was stretching his body out on a torture rack. He twisted and turned and bounced from front to back. Vague aches in the regions of his stomach and knee, caused by the situations he had found himself in over the last few days, helped to keep him awake. But it was his mind that truly gave him no peace.

Where was she? he wondered. What was she doing? Was she safe? She wasn't at the run-down hotel where she had first taken him two days before. He had checked. And the desk clerk had denied any further knowledge. For a time, Randall had driven around, looking in every nook and cranny he could find for his car, using Susan's Nissan after having collected it from the parking garage with the spare key Susan had given him.

He felt odd driving the powerful sports car, odd because he was alone. Frankie was a dominating presence even when she wasn't there. He remembered the way she had looked that first evening. He remembered the strength of his instant attraction. It had only gotten worse.

In the end, he had come back to his apartment even more confused about his feelings. But as he took time to straighten the rooms, needing the physical relief of activity, his concern for her safety had crystallized. Any city, even one as benign as San Francisco, could be unfriendly to a woman alone. He had to find her! Especially when it was his fault that she was out there on her own.

He had known that she was protective of her brother. Look what she was doing for him, for heaven's sake! Yet Randall still had attacked, accusing Michael of putting her at risk, of being stupid in his actions. And even if that was true, what had he expected her to do? Thank him?

And Susan. The solemn-faced little girl who had clung to him for love and assurance after the death of her parents. If everything turned out all right, he would get closer to Susan again. Once, he had thought he was close to her, but he must have missed something along the way. Her life had taken at least two important turns that he had known nothing about.

Why had she left him so completely in the dark? What were her plans now that she planned to marry? Did she plan to finish at the university? He didn't know! Why hadn't she told him? He wasn't some sort of ogre who would disapprove of everything she might want to do, the kind of man that Frankie's grandfather was. He had listened to her, tried to encourage her. So why had she not confided in him? And why had Frankie run away?

Randall rolled onto his side and stared at the wall in the moonlight. The light of a new day couldn't come fast enough for him.

RANDALL HAD JUST completed the finishing touches of his toilette. He'd smoothed his hair into its accustomed style, adjusted the collar of his shirt—his *own* shirt—and had inserted his contact lenses, when the doorbell rang.

When he awakened early this morning from a light doze, the first thought that had occurred to him was to check the San Francisco telephone directory for Frankie's listing. Maybe she, like him, had decided to return to her own apartment for the night. Unable to wait, he had found her name. But all that was listed was a telephone number. No address. He had tried the number, but the call wasn't answered. Today, he planned to take a leaf from her book and go to the library to search a reverse directory for her address.

The doorbell rang again before Randall could answer it. He had no idea who it might be. Was it one of the hooligans coming back to do more damage? He opened the door carefully, only to see Frankie standing on the doorstep!

She, too, had changed into clothing that probably more accurately reflected her normal life. She wore a trim, blue skirt and a white blouse along with a fitted jacket that still managed to look very feminine. Her pale blond hair feathered around her face as it had before, but it had a little more height, as if she had done more with it than just let it dry in place. Her makeup was applied with a more subtle hand, too, emphasizing rather than overwhelming her features.

Her attitude hadn't changed, though. She cocked a hand on one hip and said without preamble, "They want to see you, too. I tried to talk them out of it, but they wouldn't listen. Can you be ready in ten minutes?" She came into the apartment and looked around, but she made no comment.

Randall had to remind himself to close the door. He had been so worried for her, unable to sleep. But now that she was here and safe, he felt the old frustration begin to grow, as well as his impotent anger. She seemed to enjoy making life difficult for him! "Where were you last night?" he demanded. "I tried to find you."

"I went back to my apartment."

"How did you find me?"

"Your friends. The ones who own the place where we stayed."

"You've been over there?" He glanced at his watch. It was barely nine o'clock.

"I got them out of bed, but they were very nice about it."

Randall groaned.

"I picked up my suitcase while I was there and your thrift-store clothes. Do you want them?"

"If I never see them again—" Randall began.

"Philip Massey agreed to meet with us at nine-thirty. Actually he *expects* to meet with us at nine-thirty. It's sort of a command performance."

Randall frowned. "Do you think he knows we have the tape?"

"Probably. Their organization is like some kind of science-fiction monster with feelers all over the place. They probably even know you have it in your safe. That's why he insisted that you be present, too."

She seemed in no mood for softness. A brittle edge carried her forward. It was as if she was driving herself, afraid that if she let down her guard, there might be no getting it back up again. Her gaze flickered over him. "Are you ready?"

"Just about," he said.

She looked at her watch.

Randall took the hint. He went back into his bedroom. He was fully dressed, but he wanted to get something.

Randall didn't like violence, but he wasn't against defending himself or the people that he cared about. He found one of the rolls of coins he kept handy for change and slipped it into his jacket pocket. From somewhere, he'd heard that a coin roll made an excellent addition to a clenched fist. He thought he'd bring it along. Just in case.

THE HOTEL IN WHICH the Massey brothers were quartered was one of San Francisco's finest. As she crossed the cavernous lobby with Randall, Francesca's instinct was to turn and run. Maybe there was some other way!

She glanced at Randall, who walked coolly and confidently at her side. He wasn't wearing his glasses this morning. She could see his eyes without hindrance, and he didn't look overly concerned. But she was. What if Philip Massey reacted angrily? What if he took his anger out on them?

A man stepped forward. "Francesca James?" he asked gruffly.

Francesca nodded. She tried not to tremble. She tried to retain her impassive expression.

"And is this Mr. Peters?" The man directed his attention to Randall.

Randall answered. "It is."

The man smiled. He was tall and thin and looked like everyone's idea of an accountant. He might have been one, but Francesca doubted it. He said, "Come with me, please," and turned toward the elevators.

Francesca started to follow, but was temporarily detained by Randall. He held her back and whispered, "For once, let me do most of the talking. This is my turf. I know what I'm doing here. I'm *paid* by people to negotiate." His gray eyes were intent. Once again, she nodded.

Their escort whistled as they were lifted to the proper floor, and he smiled when he noticed that Francesca was looking at him. It was a creepy feeling, because the smile never managed to reach his eyes.

Francesca was first off the elevator. She held her chin high, but her knees were quaking.

"Right this way," the man said, motioning for them to precede him.

Two oversize men stood outside a door at the far end of the hall, guarding entry to a specially reserved set of suites that could be sealed off from the rest of the hotel. The sentinels didn't look very friendly, and both were built like weight lifters. Very politely, they asked Francesca for her purse and her jacket, then turned Randall to the wall and gave him a proper frisking.

"What's this?" one of them asked, drawing back. He withdrew the roll of coins from Randall's pocket.

"It's for parking," Randall explained.

"Maybe," the man said, smiling slightly. "You don't mind if I keep this here, do you?"

Randall shrugged. "No. Why should I?"

After being checked, Francesca's purse and jacket were handed back to her, and the 'accountant' knocked once on the door. It was promptly opened by yet another man. This one was young and slim and barely out of his teens.

They were led into one of the suites. A man was sitting on the sofa, a golden robe wrapped about his chubby body. At his side was a giant vase of freshly arranged flowers. In front of him was a tray containing what was left of an extravagant breakfast. Philip Massey watched as they crossed the room, but took the time necessary to finish his meal before addressing them. After waving them to a pair of chairs, he sat back like a king as the younger man removed the tray.

Massey's round head was covered with a fuzz of dark brown hair, his cheeks were soft and seemingly hairless, and his eyes were blue slits of estimation. "So," he said in a voice that was oddly thin but still had the power to send chills down Francesca's spine. "You have the tape." It was a statement, not a question.

Francesca met his gaze bravely, while Randall relaxed into his seat and crossed a leg, to give the illusion of confidence. "We do," he said, and said no more.

A silent battle of wills was waged at that point, each man waiting for the other to speak. The 'accountant' shifted slightly in the background. Francesca's heart pounded.

"I'd like it back," Philip Massey said simply after several moments passed.

"My client refuses," Randall said.

"Then your client is a fool. His career is over!"

Randall sat forward. "Wasn't that the idea all along? Michael James merely safeguarded his creation."

"We have a contract!"

"My client's contract was with Glass House Records."

"Which my brother and I now own."

"The contract was executed before the takeover. If we have to, we'll go to court to gain a release. We'll present the case to a judge and see what he has to say."

Massey turned to Francesca, his small eyes boring into her. "Your brother must be persuaded to see reason. Tell him that if he comes to me, we will talk . . . work everything out."

"Don't you mean *you'll* talk and *he'll* listen?" she challenged. "And will you guarantee that he'll come out of the meeting in exactly the same condition as he went in? I don't trust you, Mr. Massey. I don't trust you any farther than I can throw you."

Randall raised a quelling hand. "My client will agree to a meeting only on the condition that it take place in my office. If that's not satisfactory, then we'll see you in court." Randall smiled. "You're a businessman, Mr. Massey. A good one, from everything I've heard. You know when to hedge a bet and when to play it. Michael James is a very talented musician, one that I believe you've expressed an interest in before and undoubtedly one that you still have an interest in. I see no reason why a fair settlement can't be worked out."

Philip Massey looked at Randall from beneath half-closed eyelids. His gaze switched to Francesca. His lips curled into a semblance of a smile. "Tell your brother I agree. Of course, my brother and I will be adequately represented."

"Of course," Randall concurred. "I'll contact you about a time."

The man signaled to his assistant. The young man hurried over, motioned Randall and Frankie to their feet, then scooted them out the door, all without saying a word. At the exit into the hall, the two sentries parted, allowing them to pass. Then the 'accountant' gave that cold smile that never reached his eyes and quietly closed the door behind them.

They started to walk away. "Aren't you forgetting something?" one of the burly sentinels called to Randall. He laughed as he tossed the roll of coins.

"What was that about?" Francesca murmured as they continued down the hall.

Randall shook his head. He didn't want to talk about it. He already felt ridiculous enough.

At the portico outside the hotel, Randall paused, unsure of their next step. He didn't know if Frankie approved of the way he had handled the initial negotiation, but he felt he had gained at least one substantial concession in getting the Masseys to agree to talk.

He turned toward her, thinking to mention his satisfaction, when she surprised him by saying, "I think I know where Michael and Susan are."

He stared at her. "You do? Where?"

"I spoke with Marc. He told me."

An unreasoning shaft of jealousy shot through Randall. Was that really where she had spent last night? With Marc? She hadn't been in her apartment as she claimed, not unless she'd just neglected to answer her phone early this morning. His reply was derisive. "Was he sober?"

"As a judge."

That answer did little to assure Randall of anything. Not when he was personally aware of the drinking habits of certain judges. But he shrugged the thought aside. "Then we'd better go talk to them. Tell them what's happening. I'd like a chance to consult with Michael, and I also want to examine a copy of his contract."

"Michael won't want to meet with them," she said. "He probably won't do it."

"Then it will be up to you to persuade him, just like that guy upstairs said. Michael can't stay in hiding forever. Not if he wants any kind of a life ... not to mention a career. And he can't expect Susan to give up her life to stay with him."

"I didn't say *I* wanted that," she replied. "I'm just telling you what he'll say. He's a very stubborn person sometimes."

"Just like his sister."

"I'm not stubborn," she denied hotly. Then her features softened as she conceded, "Well, not always."

Smiling, too, Randall waved to a doorman to retrieve the Nissan. The man signaled the car forward and pocketed the tip. Randall had no doubt that Frankie would go with him.

The house where Michael and Susan were reported to be staying was close to the Pacific. It was one of many similar houses that were lined closely together along a well-kept street. Small gardens were located in the rear yards, and most houses boasted an individual garage, which allowed parking along the street to be no problem.

"You're not going to hit him or anything, are you?" Frankie asked as she got out of the car. Randall stared at her. "Because of everything that's happened," she explained. "He doesn't even know you except for what Susan's said."

"Hold it." Randall drew her around before they started up the pathway. "I want you to answer to something before we go inside. You owe me that much."

"What is it?" she asked, the china blue eyes wide and curious.

"Exactly how did Susan meet your brother?"

Frankie's hesitation was barely perceptible. "Through me."

"You?"

She nodded. "Susan was a student in a special course at the university. It's taught by the sociology professor I work for. He's involved in a study to try to find a solution to the problems of the homeless. A lot of research is involved, and Susan was one of the volunteers."

"Susan?"

"I know." She smiled slightly. "She's always liked her creature comforts. She told me that. But it's precisely because of that attitude that she learned so much. It's something that happens frequently when people begin to see the homeless as real people with real problems, not just as street scum who won't try. I don't care how many television shows or documentaries a person watches, it doesn't really hit home until you're on the street yourself, working with the people and talking with them. You learn, even if you're just passing out food.''

''Which is how she met Anne LeBaron.''

Francesca nodded.

''But I still don't see how she and Michael—''

''Michael helped out from time to time, too. You should listen to some of his songs. Then you'd understand. Michael isn't what you said he was. He might make mistakes in judgment at times, but his mistakes come straight from the heart.''

''I'll have to buy his album.''

''If it ever gets made.''

''It will.''

THE HOUSE SEEMED TO BE deserted. No one answered their knock. If Susan and Michael were alone, neither would come to the door.

Frankie led the way toward the fenced backyard.

''Be careful in case there's a dog,'' Randall warned, following closely behind her.

She rattled the gate before opening it. There were no barks. She opened it and went inside.

Bits and pieces of someone's life were scattered about the tiny lawn. There was an old metal chair, a collapsed swing set and several stacks of galvanized pipe. The grass was high.

"Do you know this place?" Randall asked.

"No."

"I hope Marc knew what he was talking about. Just how drunk was he when you talked to him? Drunk enough to get the address wrong?"

"No, I told you. He was sober. What you saw the other night wasn't the real him. He was upset. Worried about Michael. He escaped the only way he knew how."

"Stop defending him," he instructed.

"Stop making me!" she returned.

When they arrived at the back porch, Frankie stepped up to the door and knocked, calling softly, "Michael, it's me, Frankie. It's almost over, Michael. Randall's found a way. He's here with me, too. Please let us in."

A curtain moved nearby, drawing Randall's eye. He thought he saw a flash of brown hair. Susan? The door opened a crack, hesitated, then opened wider.

"Frankie?" a soft musical baritone inquired. It was followed by the slender frame of a young man with curling brown hair and a thin, aesthetic face. A wide smile broke over his features when he saw that his visitor really was his sister. From the edge of the door frame, Susan peeked outside, too. Seeing Randall, she launched herself into his arms, making the same tiny squeaking sound she had as a child when she was especially pleased about something.

Brothers and sisters hugged each other, then Susan transferred herself to Frankie's arms. Great tears rolled down her cheeks as she laughed and cried.

Randall and Michael viewed each other over the top of the women's heads, taking stock, reserving a decision on friendship. Susan settled beneath Michael's arm, clinging to his waist while wiping at her cheeks. After all the strain, they were still a pair. Both wore ragged jeans, faded T-shirts and were barefoot.

"We'd better not be out here long," Michael said, urging them into the house and looking furtively behind them as they went.

"Did you hear what I said before, Michael?" Francesca asked once they had all collected in a dimly lit living room. "It's almost over. Randall and I talked to Philip Massey. They're willing to work out a deal."

"If I do that, I'm dead," Michael said flatly.

"Not in my office, you won't be," Randall contradicted.

"It won't make any difference! It would be the same thing as committing suicide!"

"Not if you agree to work for them," Randall suggested, drawing three shocked looks.

"No!" Michael cried.

"You can't mean that!" Susan said, staring at her brother as if he had betrayed them. "If you do, you just don't understand the situation at all, Randall."

"I understand a lot more than you think I do. You can't go on hiding forever. Surely you must see that by now. What kind of life is it to be afraid to go outside your own door. And it's not even your door, is it? This house belongs to someone else. Frankie tells me that you want to get married. What about kids? Are you going to keep them hidden, too? And where's the money going to come from to support you? Savings can't last forever. Neither will your friends' generosity."

"That's not true!" Susan said in denial, but tears had again flooded her eyes.

Randall went on. "The only solution I see is to get the Masseys on your side and bury the differences between you. Let pure economics drive the marketplace. They're *not* going to kill someone who's capable of laying a golden egg for them. They know you're talented. That's why they wanted you in the first place. Now they want the master. So that means they've heard how good the tape is. Otherwise, they wouldn't care. Let them have it—along with a number of contractual provisions to protect yourself. Renegotiate. Make the situation work for *you*. Right now, you don't have the money to buy your way out of this. Bide your time. You won't be binding yourself to them forever. We'll make sure of that. You can get out of it in a year or two."

Two pairs of china blue eyes had fastened on him, as well as Susan's darker gray eyes. For a moment, no one said anything. Then Michael said, "I'm beginning to see what you mean, but—"

The door behind them burst open and three men rushed into the room. In reaction, Susan screamed and

Michael swore. Frankie darted a frightened look toward Randall. Two of the men were the pair who had been following them all along. The other was one of the massively built sentinels who had guarded Philip Massey's door. They had been followed! Double-crossed! Philip Massey must have agreed to a meeting only to throw them off guard. They had led the men directly to Michael!

Everyone seemed to act at once. Susan tightened her hold on Michael's arm just as Michael tried to peel her loose so that he could defend himself with her at a safe distance. Frankie sprang forward, screeching her anger. She attacked the first man she came to—the sentinel—and was roughly shoved aside, a plaything to the man's strength. She crashed awkwardly to the floor, but was on her feet again in a flash.

Randall searched his pocket for the roll of coins, at last finding a use for them. Then making a fist around their width, he weighed in with an uppercut to the sentinel's jaw. The man dropped like a felled tree. Randall stared at him until Frankie grabbed his arm, directing his attention to the two other men.

"No! *No!*" Susan cried, batting at the hands that tried to catch hold of her. She had been pushed into a corner, separated from Michael, who at the moment was holding his own with his assailant. Randall rushed to his sister's aid, hitting out at the tall, thin man from the Cadillac. The man laughed as he evaded every blow.

Frankie helped her sibling by breaking a wooden chair across the shorter man's back, distracting him from his attack. Blood ran down Michael's cheek, and when she saw it, her anger increased.

Finally Randall knocked the tall man down, rendering him unconscious with another well-placed uppercut. He called to Susan, but she seemed paralyzed, unable to move. But upon spying the blood that trickled down the side of her lover's face, she recovered from her daze to whisper brokenly, "Michael?"

Randall moved into the fray between Frankie and the shorter man. Built like a stump, he was tremendously strong. A blow from Randall's fortified fist directly on his jaw seemed nothing more than a gentle love pat. Then Randall switched to pummeling him in the stomach, partially in hope of weakening him, and partially in repayment for his own previous injuries at this man's hands.

The continued pounding served only to make the man angry. Like a bull, he bellowed when Michael hit the end of his nose, and he bellowed again when Francesca cuffed his ear.

Randall was drawing back, preparing to deliver what he hoped would be the telling blow, when he sensed that someone had come up behind him. He wondered vaguely if it was Susan coming to help him. But he never had a chance to find out. The last thing he remembered before knowing no more was the stricken look on Frankie's face as her gaze focused on someone standing just beyond his shoulder.

Chapter Thirteen

Francesca watched with horror as Randall crumpled at her feet.

The taller man from the Cadillac had shaken off Randall's blow and had come to settle the score. He had used no weapon, merely clasped fingers that he had brought down with force on the back of Randall's neck. The man smiled, proud of himself. "I never did like him," he explained calmly, "even before I found out that he was a lawyer."

"You bastard," Francesca ground out.

The man's smile increased. "That's something else I like, a woman with an attitude."

From the corner of her eye, Francesca saw Susan's steady approach. She had gone into the kitchen and had found a heavy, iron frying pan. It was raised into position above her head.

Francesca tossed her own head, keeping the man's attention solely upon herself. She could hear the scuffle still going on between Michael and the shorter thug. Michael wasn't nearly as strong, but he was more agile. Somehow, he was managing to hold his own. "Well, I don't like you," she said. "And I don't like the man you work for, either. He's about as trustworthy as a snake!"

"He won't like hearing—"

There was a dull clang as the frying pan collided with the tall man's skull. He collapsed like a rag doll, his eyes glazing over in surprise.

Susan stared at him. "Did I kill him?" she whispered.

Francesca didn't particularly care. Later on, she might again feel compassion. At present, she had to help her brother. She pulled the pan from Susan's hands and stalked over to the shorter man, who had straddled Michael's prone body and was hitting him repeatedly. The man looked around just in time to see his fate. In the next second he, too, was spread-eagle on the floor, just a few inches away from Randall.

"Are you all right?" Francesca asked Michael, who was struggling to sit up. He had collected other cuts and bruises, the most immediate, a tear near the corner of his eye that he was testing gingerly.

Susan ran to his side, fell to her knees and wrapped her arms around his neck.

Francesca surveyed the scene around her. The sentinel was still unconscious by the sofa, the larger thug was arranged in a sort of ball, and the shorter thug was supine at her feet. And Randall was lying motionless, his long body awkwardly twisted, a roll of coins not far from his hand.

As Susan openly wept, Francesca stood rigidly in place. If Randall had been badly hurt, it was her fault. From the first moment, she had not given a thought to the danger she was placing him in. She had been concerned only for Michael and for what she wanted done in order to help him. What Randall thought, what he felt meant nothing. She hadn't asked him to help; she had told him that he would. She had ridiculed him, just to get him to do as she wished.

Susan cried out her brother's name, transferring her ministrations to him. "Randall!" she called, "Randall!" Turning him over, she pushed the light brown hair away from his brow with trembling fingers.

He moved slightly, groaning. His eyelids fluttered open. When his gaze cleared, it was fixed on Francesca.

Susan's laughter was shaken. "Oh, thank God! You're all right! For a little while, I thought— Oh, Randall. I'm so sorry I was mean to you. I know you were only trying to do your best."

Randall sat up, grabbing at the back of his neck and groaning once again as he did. Slowly he became aware of the fallen men scattered around him. "Good grief," he muttered.

The closest man started to stir, causing Randall to stagger to his feet. Still shaken, he extended a hand to his prospective brother-in-law to assist him from the floor. "We'd better get out of here, don't you think?"

"Is it safe to leave?" Michael asked, swaying slightly in place.

"Safer than staying here," Randall replied.

Francesca's emotions felt numbed. She moved when they moved, got into the car when they did, and she even listened to their conversation, but she didn't take part.

"What do we do now?" Michael asked. He and Susan occupied the back seat of the Nissan. Susan refused to drive because she was too upset. Her head was buried in the hollow between Michael's chest and his shoulder, and he held on to her tightly, as if for reassurance... for both of them.

Randall glanced away from the road. Francesca felt his gaze fall on her, but she didn't respond. "I suppose that depends on you," he said to Michael. "What do you think we should do?"

Michael sighed, running a hand through his curling hair. "All I want is for this to be over!"

"How do you feel about what I said earlier?"

"You mean about renegotiating my contract? Do you still think that's possible? Even after this? They tried to kill us back there!"

Randall disagreed. "If they'd meant to kill us, we wouldn't be here talking. I didn't see any weapons, did you? *Think*, Michael. The Massey brothers are nasty, unscrupulous people. But do you truly believe they'd risk everything they've built up on a murder conviction? I doubt it. They're bullies. They like to throw their weight around, beat people up, frighten them and even destroy some careers along the way. But they're not stupid. They're *far* from stupid.

"Like I said before. Make the situation work for you. Maybe they did take over Glass House Records so Philip Massey could get at you, but they also got a pretty sweet deal out of it according to Frankie. Glass House was in financial trouble; the Masseys came in and bought it for a song. You're not the only artist Glass House has under contract, are you? There are a few others. And they got the studio, the equipment, the name—"

"And a base of operations in San Francisco," Michael said.

Randall nodded. "Exactly. If we set up the contract right, your interests will be fully protected. We'll put enough conditions in there that if they want you, they won't even be able to breathe in your face hard. Then later, if you don't like dealing with them, you can get out of it." He paused. "I know a good entertainment attorney in Los Angeles."

"You wouldn't represent me yourself? I thought Frankie said—"

"You want the best contract you can come up with, don't you? Get an expert. I'm not an expert in that field."

"You've been pretty satisfactory so far," Michael said, smiling slowly. "That was a pretty mean uppercut you threw back there."

"He had a glass jaw," Randall replied, grinning. "I barely touched him."

Again Randall glanced at Francesca, but she couldn't make herself respond. In fact, she turned farther away to stare out the window. It was over now. Everything was working out. Michael would be safe, and so would his career. Susan and he would marry. She would go back to the university and the professor she was assisting. She had gotten everything that she wanted. Life could return to normal. Or could it?

Unconsciously she drew a quick breath as something within her seemed to crack, the full horror of the past half hour exploding in her mind. She had been so afraid when the men had burst into the room and when she'd realized they had been double-crossed.

Francesca started to tremble. Delayed reaction, a medical expert might diagnose. But she knew the true cause. At the moment when dangerous men had shattered the relative peace of that little house, had she been afraid for Michael? Or had she been more afraid for someone else? Someone who, without her being aware of it, had come to hold a significant place in her heart.

Francesca didn't want to believe it. She couldn't love Randall! Love took a long time to flower and grow. It didn't exist on the stony ground of coercion and mistrust. There had been no spark, no nourishment! *She* certainly hadn't encouraged it. She didn't want to fall in love with him! Falling in love made a person vulnerable, took away her strength, made her weak. She had seen it with her mother, and she had experienced it herself. She wouldn't do it! She wouldn't let it happen! It was early on. She could nip it in the bud. They had only known each other for a few short days, even if those days did somehow feel like a lifetime.

With a steely force of will, she controlled her trembling and again put her mind to the problem of helping her brother. He wasn't out of the woods yet. He still had to deal with the Massey brothers and make them agree to his terms. He would need all the encouragement and moral support that he could get. She would try not to think of the way Randall had looked, unconscious at her feet, with his long body crumpled and possibly broken. She would try not to think of the guilt she had felt.

She wouldn't *let* herself.

RANDALL TOOK EVERYONE TO his apartment, where he made several telephone calls to locate his friend in Los Angeles. After gaining his agreement to represent Michael, Randall then placed the necessary call to Philip Massey, pressuring him into a real meeting later in the week. "He didn't sound very pleased," Randall said after hanging up. "But I think he was aware that his men had blown it. They must have had a hard time explaining."

"Good," Susan said approvingly.

"As well as headaches," Michael teased. "At least, for two of them. After Susan and Frankie got through with them."

"It was the only heavy thing I could find," Susan said defensively.

"A fry pan!" Michael grinned. The gesture hurt his bruised lip and he started, which in turn hurt his ribs and made him groan. His smile was strained as he kissed Susan's forehead. With their arms lightly encircling each other, they sat on Randall's couch. "Maybe we should ask if we can keep it. Get it bronzed and hang it in a prominent place in our living room."

"No way!" Susan shivered. "I don't want to even think of it again."

Randall's gaze settled upon Francesca, who continued to avoid looking at him. She wasn't smiling. He wasn't even sure if she was listening. At first, he had made excuses for her remoteness, thinking it due to shock. Now, he wasn't so sure.

He spoke again to the lovers. "You should keep on the safe side, though. They're probably through trying to get at you, but nothing's ever a sure bet. Frankie and I thought it was over earlier. Otherwise, we would never have come straight to the house. Isn't that right, Frankie?"

She gave a tight smile. "Of course." Her voice was cool, remote.

Randall felt a spurt of anger. What was it with her? Hadn't everything worked out exactly as she had wanted?

Francesca got stiffly to her feet. "Michael, I think we should go. We've already imposed enough."

Michael frowned, looking at his sister.

She continued. "Mr. Peters must have any number of other things to do." She turned to Randall, her face composed, and extended her hand. "I meant what I said before when I told you I wanted to pay for your time. Give Michael your charges and I'll send the money to you right away."

Randall stood up. He took her hand. Her fingers were as cold as her conduct. "Frankie—" he began.

She pulled away. "Michael?" she prompted, a brittle edge to her voice.

Michael stood, bringing Susan up with him. He was confused. He looked from Randall to his sister and then back again. Randall met the puzzlement of Michael's gaze with equal puzzlement of his own.

Susan reached out to hug her brother. "Are you sure you're all right?" she asked.

"I'm fine," Randall assured. Physically, he was. Mentally, he wasn't so sure.

Francesca had already started for the door. Michael shook Randall's hand. "Thanks for all you've done," he said. "I know we haven't had much time to get to know one another, but Susan's raved about you so much, I feel I already do."

Michael's china blue eyes, so familiar to Randall, yet set in a different face, wanted his approval. Randall didn't withhold it. He smiled and for Susan's sake added, "I'm looking forward to getting to know you, too."

Susan again hugged Randall. "I love you," she whispered in his ear. "I'll call to let you know where we are."

"You'd better," Randall warned, smiling slightly. Then he added, "And, young lady, we have to have a talk."

Susan looked uncertain for a moment before giving her brother an apologetic grin. Then she grasped Michael's hand and hurried after Francesca, who was already a distance down the hall.

Left alone, Randall could only stare at the door. She hadn't even bothered to say goodbye.

For the remainder of the afternoon, Randall allowed himself the privilege of giving in to both his aches and his anger. His body felt bruised, and for good reason. His neck felt as if a battering ram had collided with it. His head hurt. Even his teeth hurt! And Frankie hadn't seemed in the least concerned. Now that his usefulness was over, he might have become invisible. No "thank you," no "I hope you haven't been hurt too badly." Just "figure up your bill and I'll pay it." Wouldn't she be surprised if he actually did send a statement? He could mention his battered body, kidnapping, coercion, reckless endangerment and theft. She would be lucky if he didn't prosecute!

And he had wondered if he might be falling in love with her. Impossible! He was glad to be rid of her, glad to get back to his regular life.

Randall packed an ice bag for his sore neck, stretched out on his bed and tried to forget that he had ever been attracted to her, even in the slightest. He didn't like blue eyes. He didn't like short, blond hair. He didn't like women who were barely five feet tall and built with exquisite care. And he damned well didn't like dimples!

THE FEAT OF FORGETTING Frankie was easier said than done, a fact Randall realized during the next couple of weeks as he stumbled through what once had been routine. He couldn't seem to get the proper handle on anything anymore. People said what he expected them to say and did what he expected them to do. No one acted at all out of the ordinary. There were no surprises. Not that he wanted surprises, it was just… He became impatient at the oddest moments. Restless. His mind wandered. When he was least prepared, he thought of her. And that was something he definitely did not want to do! But he seemed to have no control left. Not even in the company of his friends.

Paul watched Randall from the other side of the table at the end of a special meal Allison had prepared one evening.

Allison, too, looked at him speculatively. "Randall?" she said in her quiet voice. "Do you want to talk to us about something? We're your friends. We'll do anything to help you."

Randall jumped, dropping the spoon he'd been swirling in his coffee for God knew how long.

"It's nothing," he said. " Just—"

Her hand came out to cover his, and he looked up into the beautiful, pale face that was dominated by warm green eyes and an abundance of shoulder-length, red-gold hair. The sweetness and generosity of her spirit showed through in her smile. "It's not nothing," she contradicted, her voice soft. She glanced at Paul for encouragement and continued. "You've been on edge ever since we came back from our honeymoon. Sometimes, you cover it better than others, but—Randall, let us help. Please? Is it that girl? The one who woke us up a couple of weeks ago? Paul thinks you love her."

"Paul talks too much," Randall grumbled, shooting his friend a pointed look.

Allison smiled. "Don't be angry with him. I made him tell me. I've been worried about you." She paused. "She seemed very sweet."

Randall snorted. "I wouldn't choose that word to describe her."

"What word would you choose, then?" Paul asked.

"I'd rather not think about it that much."

"But you can't stop, right?"

Randall stood up and unconsciously began to pace. Paul and Allison exchanged glances.

"Randall," Allison said, getting up to stop him. "Why don't we take our coffee into the living room? Then we can talk. I really think you need to. You helped Paul and me so much when we needed it. You helped with Grandfather... and that meant so much, especially close to the end."

"I liked your grandfather."

"I know. And he would have liked you, too, if he'd been aware." She gave a tiny sigh. Paul moved up behind her and placed his hands on her shoulders. She touched one softly before continuing. "We're so happy now, Randall. It breaks our hearts to see you unhappy."

"I'm not—" He started to deny that he was unhappy, but his throat felt thick. He stopped. He couldn't lie to them. Just as he couldn't continue to lie to himself. "All right," he said. "Let's talk. But I doubt it will do any good."

"That's what I like," Paul quipped, "an optimist, right from the start!"

Randall smiled, but it wasn't deeply felt.

An hour later, his words came to a halt. Both Paul and Allison had been held fascinated, laughing at some parts of his tale and watching him very seriously at others.

"That's it," Randall said. "That's the whole story."

"Aren't you forgetting something?" Paul reminded him.

"What?"

"Well, to hear you tell it, there was no physical attraction between you. Somehow I just don't believe it."

"There was attraction," Randall admitted.

"Which neither of you acted upon...?" A tinge of guilty color stole into Randall's cheeks. Paul's smile was pleased. "I thought so."

"It didn't mean anything."

Paul swallowed his disbelief but it was evident all the same.

Allison, curled on the couch at her husband's side, asked, "And she just walked away? She didn't say anything to you after you were hit?"

"She asked for my bill and called me 'Mr. Peters.'"

Allison was silent a moment before drawing a deep breath. "Randall, you always give people good advice. Are you willing to receive some yourself."

"I *used* to give good advice. Now—" He shook his head, doubtfully.

"Go talk to her," Allison urged. "You won't have anything to lose. At worst, you'll see that she doesn't interest you anymore. At best—well, at best, you'll be as happy as Paul and I are. I hope you won't hate us for interfering, but I seem to remember a little interference from you when things were a little iffy in our relationship."

"A lot of interference," Paul corrected. "He made a date with you and then told me I was keeping it."

"But I knew you two loved each other. This is different."

Allison smiled and said softly, "Maybe it's not so different after all."

Chapter Fourteen

Francesca buried herself in the small office she called her own. Reams of papers and computer printouts almost dwarfed her desk, while books of all sizes and thicknesses were piled about. The world of learning had always been her escape, and she clung to it now with a stubbornness that she knew others would think amazing. She didn't have Michael's future to worry about any longer. The meeting to renegotiate his contract with the Masseys had been held and he had come out of it in a much better position than he thought possible. The lawyer from Los Angeles had been wonderful, Michael had said. So had Randall, he'd added, but Francesca had cut him off. She hadn't wanted to hear about Randall. She had enough trouble keeping him out of her mind without Michael singing his praises.

She plunged into her work, losing herself in statistics and the stories of other people's lives, aching at the unfairness of the plight of so many of them. When a tap sounded on the open door of her office, she looked up to find Michael standing there, grinning. In his hand was the award he had won the previous night. It had been presented by one of the music industry's fan magazines for Most Promising New Artist of the Year.

"Well? What do you think?" he asked, his grin widening so far that he could barely contain it.

Francesca lowered her pencil and beamed back. "It's absolutely the most wonderful award I've ever seen."

He brushed an imaginary speck of dust away from the rounded glass surface. "It is rather nice, isn't it? I think I'll build it a showcase with three... no two of those small spotlights. I wouldn't want to seem too ostentatious."

Francesca laughed. "You idiot. Let me see."

As his sister examined the award, Michael hitched a seat on the only empty corner of her desk.

"It's beautiful, Michael," she said. "Truly beautiful. Did you have any idea?"

"Absolutely none. I was so busy trying to protect Susan's and my skin, I didn't remember that I was even nominated."

"Next year... Best Performer! When does the new album come out?"

"In a few weeks. I'm really excited about it. The Masseys are, too. Philip called me in the other day, shook my hand, told me we should let bygones be bygones and even asked me out to lunch. Can you believe that?"

"Did you go?"

"What, me? Turn down a free meal?"

Francesca laughed again, shaking her head.

Michael looked about the cluttered office and at the pile of papers on his sister's desk. "Wow!" he said with a sigh. "I don't know how you stand it. I'd go bonkers in about a week."

"I love it."

"I know. Still—" He held his thought.

Francesca met his suddenly serious expression. "I *do* love it," she repeated.

Michael's eyes narrowed as they traveled over her pale face and tired eyes. "I worry about you sometimes, Frankie," he said quietly. "I worry that you'd rather be in the world of books than in the real one."

"That's not true!" Francesca denied hotly. "I live in the real world. It doesn't get more real than what I went through looking for you!"

"I know, and I'm sorry it happened. I've already told you that. It's just—this isn't *life!* You read about other people's lives and talk to them, but you don't have a life of your own."

"How do you know?" she demanded. "I don't tell you everything. You're my brother, but that doesn't mean—"

"It took me a while to figure out, but I finally did. You're in love with Randall Peters, aren't you? I couldn't believe it when you were so rude to him at his apartment, especially after everything he'd done for us. That was something so out of character."

"I don't love Randall Peters!" she cried, flushing slightly.

Her brother smiled. "They kind of sneak up on you, don't they? I didn't know I loved Susan, either, until she told me I did. Then I thought, 'Hey, I do!'"

Francesca attempted to prod Michael from his perch on her desk. "I've got work to do. If you're just going to sit there talking drivel..."

Michael laughed, allowing her to move him. Several college students passed by in the hall outside Francesca's office. One happened to look inside, and when she saw Michael, she gave a quick double take. She then whispered something to her friends and after being delegated as spokesperson, she approached the doorway.

"Excuse me," she said, "but are you Michael James?"

Michael had started to receive a great deal more attention from the media in the past week and a half. The Massey brothers' public relations machine had shifted into high gear. His picture had even been in the morning newspaper along with an interview and a mention of his prize. Still new to fame, Michael grinned. "I certainly am."

A wave of emotion broke over the girl as excitement overwhelmed restraint. "It is him! It's *him,*" she squealed. She waved to the other students. They all rushed into the room. A second group of students discovered what was going on and soon, a throng had converged in Francesca's office. Michael had been backed against the desk. He was laughing, signing autographs and answering questions. The crowd continued to grow as word spread. Gauging by the reaction, the new album was going to be a smash hit.

Francesca gave up trying to get back to work. She protected Michael's award, provided slips of paper for him to sign and in general, enjoyed the fact that he was on top of the world. The smile he gave her, not to mention the quick kiss on the cheek, included her in his exhilaration.

RANDALL ARRIVED ON CAMPUS, located the proper building and was in time to witness the mayhem. He had to replay the room number through his mind a couple of times before believing that he was at the correct place. A line had formed down the hallway. Excited voices rose and fell.

Responding to his suit and bearing, the students parted to let him into the office, thinking that he belonged there, he supposed. Inside, there was even more chaos. The office was so small that there was barcly room to turn around in the first place. Now, there was barely enough room to breathe. That small fact didn't seem to bother anyone in line, though. Then Randall saw the reason for all the excitement. Michael James was signing autographs.

The young man seemed to be enjoying it, but his smile was becoming strained. At his side, Francesca was frantically answering questions and at the same time, trying to keep order on her desk and in her surroundings. "Please," he heard her say, "don't knock the books off—Watch out for—Yes, the new album will be out soon. In a few weeks. Please be careful of—"

Randall realized that the situation was getting out of hand. In a loud voice he said, "This is enough! Out! Everyone out!" He used his best professorial tone. For a moment, everyone froze, then with added emphasis, he repeated, "I said *out!*" The crush of fans started to disperse, pushing against those behind them, slowly emptying the room.

Randall followed them into the hall, shooing away stragglers. "Go to class! Do your homework! Don't hang about!" he ordered.

When he came back into the room, he closed the door and leaned back against it, laughing at the absurdity of his impersonation. Both Michael and Francesca stared at him. "You looked like you needed help," he explained. "Did I do the wrong thing?"

Michael was first to speak. "Oh, wow, no! It was fun at first, but—I've never had anything like that happen before. A few people here and there when we were playing at a club. But never this!"

"Get used to it. I saw your interview this morning. Congratulations."

"Thanks." Michael ran a hand through his curly hair in a gesture of relief. "Thanks for more than one reason. I was afraid what was going to happen next!"

Randall's gaze settled on Francesca, who continued to stare at him as if he were an apparition. She blinked when she realized that he was looking back at her and quickly turned away.

Michael followed the unspoken interaction. He drew himself up. "Do you think they'll still be out there?" he asked, indicating the hall.

Randall opened the door. The coast was clear in both directions. "Seem not to be," he said.

Michael grinned. "I'd better start wearing track shoes. Just in case I have to run." He extended a hand to Randall. "See you around soon, right?"

"Right," Randall agreed. Francesca was still turned away from him.

Michael rescued his award from the desk and bent to kiss his sister's cheek. When he started for the door, Francesca stirred herself to call, "Michael, there's another way out of the building. The back way. Go through the first door on your right down the hall, follow that hall a way, then turn right again. Eventually you'll come to an exit sign."

"Thanks, sis," Michael said. He winked at her before slipping quietly from the room.

Francesca busied herself with straightening her desk, moving stacks of papers and putting books back in order. Finally when the weight of Randall's gaze got to be too much for her, she reacted with typical aggression. "What is it that you want here? Why did you come? I told you to tell Michael what your bill was. I never heard, so I couldn't pay." She reached for her purse in a lower drawer and dropped it angrily on the desktop. "Is that what this is all about? A personal dun?"

"I never gave Michael a figure because I couldn't come up with one."

"Well, I don't want to feel obligated. Here!" She scratched out a check. "That's most of my savings. I'll pay you more when I get my next check." She held the check out to him, her stance demanding that he take it.

Randall merely looked at it.

"Take it!" she ordered, her eyes flashing blue fire.

"Make me," Randall replied softly.

Francesca's resolve wavered for a second, then she came around the desk and stuffed the check into the front pocket of his jacket. "There," she said, satisfied with her handiwork.

Randall removed the check and tore it into tiny bits, letting the pieces scatter on the floor.

Her jaw tightened. She collected her checkbook and wrote another, also stuffing this one into his pocket.

Again Randall tore it up.

Francesca wrote another. "I can do this all day," she warned before angrily whirling to face him.

"So can I," he said. "But you'll run out of checks before I run out of strength."

She looked at him defiantly, the third check in her hand. "If it's not money, then what is it?" she demanded. "Don't tell me you miss me, because I won't believe it!"

Randall smiled slightly. "Maybe I do."

She tore the check up herself and went back to her desk. "I don't have time for this," she declared, sitting down. She picked up a pencil and started to read through a set of papers. "Close the door on your way out."

"You'd like me to do that, wouldn't you?" he said softly. "Just turn around and walk away. Why, Frankie? What are you afraid of?"

She twitched in her chair but said nothing. Her gaze was fixed on what she was pretending to read.

Randall moved around the desk, came up behind her and leaned close. "Is it me? Men in general? Or is it *people,* plural?" He touched her shoulder lightly and she jumped. He retraced his steps to the front of the desk, leaned over it and made her look at him.

Wide, china blue eyes met his. He could see the fear behind her anger. "What are you afraid of, Frankie?" he asked softly, earnestly wanting to know.

Frankie jumped away from her desk and ran to the door. She was through it before Randall could catch up with her.

Once again, he found himself racing after her. She ran like a deer. No wonder he had a hard time. She broke into the sunshine after pushing through the front doors, not letting up in speed as she threaded her way through the slower students using the walkway. Randall's suit hampered his movement. His shoes were not meant for great traction. Curious gazes followed them. In fact, some people stopped and stared.

She was heading for the parking lot. Randall pushed himself for greater speed. He had longer legs. He was in reasonably good condition. He should be able to make up ground. But it was not until Francesca almost had a collision with a cyclist, who hadn't seen her in time to make necessary adjustments, that he did. At the site of the near collision, only Frankie's adroit move prevented catastrophe. Still, both pedestrian and cyclist went down on a grassy slope, Francesca rolling awkwardly downhill, while the cyclist who was still attached to his bike by foot bindings, landed in an inglorious heap in a flowerbed.

The cyclist was struggling to loosen his feet when Randall went rushing by. Anyone who could curse that fluently wasn't badly hurt, he decided. But Francesca lay unmoving at the base of the slope. Randall's heart stood still.

People on the sidewalk went to the cyclist's aid. He heard another come after him. "Frankie?" Randall called breathlessly as he fell to his knees at her side.

She moved, suddenly fighting to get up. He tried to contain her, but she twisted away.

The person who had been following him came up quickly beside them. "Is she okay?" the girl asked.

Blood was dribbling from a cut on Frankie's left knee. Bits and pieces of grass were tangled in her hair. Dirt was streaked across one cheek, and various scratches decorated each arm. "I'm fine!" Francesca claimed in a shaky voice. "Just fine. Leave me alone."

"I saw you running," the girl said, giving Randall a hard look. "Was he trying to hurt you?" Randall denied the accusation, but he wasn't believed. "I'm asking her," the girl said, holding her ground.

Francesca looked at Randall. He could see her mind wrestling with the decision. Finally she said, "No."

"You're sure," the girl insisted.

"Yes," Frankie confirmed.

"We should take her to the infirmary," the girl declared.

"No!" Frankie cried. "I've told you, I'm fine. All I want is to be left alone."

"Frankie, listen to reason," Randall pleaded.

She started to limp away, struggling to get back uphill.

Randall looked at the girl, who still stood quietly nearby. He shook his head and did the only thing left for him to do. He swept Frankie up into his arms and carried her back to the walkway.

By this time, the cyclist had righted his bike, made a few adjustments to his front wheel and to himself, and now was ready to move off. "Look where you're going next time," he grumbled.

"She's hurt. Can't you see?" Randall demanded, angry that the young man could be so callous.

"She could have broken both our necks!" The younger man adjusted his helmet, still frowning fiercely. Then he gave Frankie another look and asked, "Is she hurt badly? Do you want me to get help?"

"I'm fine," Frankie repeated like a demented my-
nah bird. "Just leave me alone." She fought against
Randall's hold.

He tightened his arms. "She's very sorry she made
you fall."

"I can speak for myself!"

"Tell her it's okay," the biker said. Then he was on
his bike again, pedaling away, probably glad to be free
of them.

Randall started to walk toward the parking lot.

"Randall, put me down," she ordered.

"No."

"Randall!"

"I'm taking you to my apartment."

"I don't want to go to your apartment!"

"Too bad."

She fought him all the way to the Civic. They drew
curious glances, but no one interfered.

When he placed her in the passenger seat and
strapped her in, she glared at him angrily. "I'll have
you arrested!"

Randall made no reply. He moved quickly to the
driver's side and was in time to prevent her from getting out. "Frankie, stop fighting me."

"No!"

He leaned close and planted a kiss on her parted
lips. Then he smiled at her. "I'm not taking no for an
answer. So you might as well sit there and be quiet."

She continued to glare at him, and he continued to
smile, even as he started the car and drove away.

WHEN HE BROUGHT HER INTO his apartment, her protests had taken the form of brooding withdrawal. She wouldn't look at him. She wouldn't talk to him. Randall wondered if this might all be folly, but since he had started it, he would see it through to the end.

He pulled her straight into his bathroom, sat her down on the edge of the tub and reached for a washcloth. The blood had dried on her knee, but the cut still looked angry. He dampened the cloth with warm water and carefully started to clean the area.

She sat stiffly, unyieldingly, allowing his ministrations but not acknowledging them.

"There," he said. "That looks better. It's not bad. Not deep."

He might as well have spoken to the wall. She stared at a spot beyond his shoulder.

Randall sat back on his heel and looked at her. She was just as beautiful as he remembered and just as stubborn. She didn't appreciate having the tables turned on her, being forced from her world by him.

"Would you like a Band-Aid?" he asked, hoping to compel her to answer.

She refused to speak.

"All right," he said. "If you're going to act like a baby—" He scooped her up into his arms again.

That got her attention. "I'm *not* a baby. Put me down!"

She felt good in his arms even if she didn't want to be there.

"So we're talking now!" he said exultantly.

"We have absolutely nothing to talk about!"

"I think we do," he contradicted. He carried her into his living room and deposited her on the couch.

She fussed with the hem of her skirt, using it as an excuse not to look at him.

Randall's gaze softened. If ever he had doubted his love for her, and he had, his emotions were no longer in question. Even in the face of her anger, even in the face of her rejection, he knew that he loved her. And that no matter what might come after this day, he always would. He loved the gameness of her spirit, the fierceness of her loyalty, the vulnerability that she refused to acknowledge. But it was precisely those attributes that made the path set before him more difficult.

He eased himself onto the sofa cushion closest to her and leaned forward in order to better see her face.

"Francesca . . . That is your full name, isn't it? I remember the man at the hotel calling you that. It's a beautiful name. But I like Frankie, too. They both fit."

She gave no sign that she cared.

"One's soft and evocative. The other, full of spirit and challenge."

She fidgeted lightly.

"Just like you," he continued, his voice soft and warm.

She turned to glare at him. "Get to the point! I don't like you talking about me like that!"

It was hard to withstand the fire of her eyes, but Randall knew what he had to do.

"Why not?" he asked quietly, keeping his expression light.

She turned away. "Because I don't!"

"Why not?" he repeated.

She hissed in frustration.

"Why not?" he repeated again.

The fire in her eyes grew hotter. "Are you naturally obnoxious, or are you just practicing? I *didn't* want to see you. I *didn't* want to come here. I *don't* want to talk to you. Take the hint!"

"I don't take hints very well."

"Tell me about it!"

"I love you, Frankie."

The soft words were received like a bolt of lightning from a clear sky.

She blinked, stunned. "You're mad," she whispered.

He shrugged.

She stood up. "I don't appreciate the joke, Randall. Take me back to the university. You've had your little bit of fun."

"It's no joke. I love you."

"Stop saying that!" She covered her ears with her hands.

Randall stood up, as well. She moved quickly away from him.

"I wasn't going to do anything," he protested.

"It's a mistake! You're confusing one emotion for another!"

"I'm not a boy. I don't make that kind of mistake."

"I'm not a young girl, but I've made it before. It's not very nice when everything falls apart!"

"I'd like to talk with you about that sometime."

"No!"

"Why not? What are you afraid of, Frankie? Why won't you let anyone close? Who was he? What did he do to you?"

She turned away. "He didn't *do* anything to me."

"He hurt you."

"No, *I* hurt me! I should have known better than to trust him."

"That's it, isn't it?" he said. "It all comes down to trust! You don't trust anyone, do you? Not even yourself!"

"That's not true!"

"Then tell me who you do trust. And Michael doesn't count."

Frankie broke for the door, but this time, Randall expected it. He arrived there at the same instant as she did. He bundled her into his arms, keeping her away from the doorknob.

"You've got to stop running away, Frankie!" he said as she struggled against his hold. "Not every man is like that man or like your grandfather. You say Michael was hurt by your grandfather's meanness, but Michael's worked through his hurt. You haven't!"

"You don't know anything about it!"

"Then tell me! That's why I brought you here. I want us to talk, Frankie. To try to come to some kind of understanding. I don't expect you to tell me you love me. Not today. Not even tomorrow. All I want is for us to get to know each other better. What happened before, when we were trying to find Michael, was something out of the ordinary. We learned things about each other that it takes other people years to find out. You know I'm grouchy when I'm hungry, and I know you like to tweak the devil's tail when you think you have the upper hand. I'm willing to tell you everything you want to know about me. Are you willing to do the same?"

She looked up at him, so small in his arms, yet so ready to give challenge. "I don't love you," she said tightly, the dampness of tears coming into her eyes.

"I'll accept that for now."

She twisted free of his hold, her breathing uneven, her gaze hunted.

To help ease the situation, Randall started to talk. "I'll begin with the basics. I was born in San Francisco, a little earlier than everyone planned. It was almost Christmas and I didn't want to miss the holiday. That's what my dad always used to tell me. My birthday's December 24. So I guess he was right. Shortly after I was born, we moved to Sacramento. My father was offered a job in the state attorney general's office. That's where Susan was born. Everything went along just fine. I graduated from high school, then college and law school, and I started my career. Then one day, I got this call. Our parents had been killed in a freeway accident. Susan was in the car, too, but she had been thrown free and barely had a scratch. She was thirteen, and I was twenty-eight. That was eight years ago.''

Frankie had moved behind the couch. Her fingers played nervously on the soft leather. "Susan never told me that."

"She doesn't like to talk about it. For a time, she blamed herself. I had one hell of a time trying to get her to see that it wasn't her fault that they crashed. A car jumped the median. There wasn't anything anyone could do. It was a miracle she came through alive.'' He moved away from the door, fairly confident that Francesca would no longer try to escape. "I did the best I could. I tried to help her as she grew up. So did my Aunt Minnie. I believe I've mentioned my aunt before?''

"You never said her name."

Randall grinned. "Aunt Minnie. My friends used to have fun with her name when I was a boy. She's a great lady, though. A little opinionated, but very nice. You'd like her. She'd like you, too.''

Frankie turned away. It was too soon for planned family intimacies.

"There's not much else to tell," he continued. "I've had a couple of mutually satisfactory love affairs that broke up with all parties involved still fairly friendly. Nothing serious. I never thought I loved either one of them. So you see, I do know the difference. You've seen my office. I've been with the firm for about ten years. I hope soon to be made a partner. I like what I do—'' He shrugged. ''That's about it.''

She continued to look away.

''I'm open to questions.''

None were forthcoming.

''May I ask you one?'' he asked.

She seemed to brace herself for the worst.

''Will you tell me where you got that dimple? Michael doesn't have one.''

Chapter Fifteen

The unexpectedness of the question caused Frankie to start. She looked at him, surprised. "It's— Our mother has a dimple. S-so did our grandmother," she stammered. "At least, in the picture of her, she looks like she had one."

Randall smiled. "Only the women of the family. Interesting."

He sat down, wordlessly showing confidence that she wouldn't try to run away. He saw her glance at the door, then away again. He stayed on the couch.

"Michael looks like our dad," she volunteered. "The same curly brown hair."

"You said your father was in construction?"

"He was an iron worker. He liked to work on bridges and dams. The jobs lasted longer that way."

"What happened to him?"

"He just left one morning and didn't come back. There was some kind of accident with a steel beam. It was going to hit some people and he pushed them out of the way. Only he didn't get out of the way himself."

"A hero," Randall said quietly.

She nodded. Tears again came into her eyes. "I wish he hadn't died! After that, everything went so wrong in our lives! Oh, I know. As an adult, I should wish that he had lived for himself, for his own fulfillment. I know I shouldn't be selfish. But if he had lived—" She stopped speaking and came to the chair that matched the sofa. She sat down on the edge, as if unconsciously ensuring a quick getaway. "It was so hard on my mother," she said tightly.

"And on you and Michael. Having a dead hero for a father isn't much compensation."

"I'm still proud of him!"

"I'm sure you are. You should be."

She drew a deep breath. "Our grandfather said he was stupid. That he should have thought of his family before he did what he did. He said he was stupid, too, for not saving any money, for spending it all on frivolous things for my mother. Maybe that's true. But I'm glad he did it. I'm glad he made my mother happy! At least she *was* happy once in her life!" Francesca lapsed into silence, a captive of the past.

Randall asked softly, "Is your mother happy now?"

"No."

"Why doesn't she leave, then? What makes her stay with him?"

"I've asked her to come live with me, but she won't! She just stays there, taking that man's abuse—"

Frankie got up, but she didn't head for the door. "She says it's because she loves him, but—"

Randall was very careful in what he said next. "Is he ill? Is that why she stays?"

"He's too mean to be ill. No self-respecting virus would hang around long enough to—" Her words broke off. Her features were still.

Randall rose slowly and covered the distance between them. When he first reached out to her, she turned away. The second time he reached for her, she let his hands find purchase on her shoulders. "Frankie, look at me," he said, pulling her around.

Huge, china blue eyes raised to his; her expression was so much like a wounded child's that Randall felt his throat tighten.

"You are *not* your mother. You don't have to prove how strong you are, or how brave. Your mother stays with your grandfather for her own reasons. They.have nothing to do with you. They never did."

"I love her," she said, her voice trembling.

"I'm sure you do. But it would also be natural for you to be angry with her for exposing you and Michael to your grandfather's venom for all those years."

"I love her!"

"I know."

"She did the best she could under very difficult circumstances!"

He watched her closely. "If you had a child, would you let him stay with your grandfather?"

"No!" Her voice broke. Then, so did her control. The tears that had threatened twice before fell in a mounting torrent. She covered her face and let her head drop forward onto Randall's chest. As gently as he could, he gathered her into his arms.

Minutes passed. Frankie didn't move. The front of Randall's shirt became damp, but he didn't care. It was a small price to pay for getting to the root of a problem. Especially a problem that could directly affect his future happiness. He had been right when he'd wondered if her mother's inability to break away from her own father's domination had placed at risk the emotional lives of her children. It had.

Frankie went through life unconsciously thinking that she had to prove herself, to show that she wasn't weak like her mother. Already independent by the time they'd gone to live with her grandfather, she'd had to watch the way her mother let him verbally abuse them all. When her mother had done nothing constructive to stop him, it must have been hard for Frankie to deal with, both as a child and as an adult.

He didn't want to change Frankie; he loved everything about her just as she was. He loved her independent spirit, her way of taking on the world. But for her sake, he wanted her to see clearly what was happening—that she didn't have to prove anything to anyone, especially herself.

Also, she had to be able to trust again. She had to trust that the person closest to her wouldn't betray her, wouldn't be strong one moment and weak the next, and would stand up for her forever. No matter what.

She moved restively in his arms. With some reluctance, Randall let her go. He found a tissue for her to wipe her eyes with, and she accepted it with a solemn little smile. "I didn't mean for that to happen," she said, embarrassed. "I don't know why I did it. I don't normally cry."

"Susan says a good cry is equal to at least three Snickers bars," he teased.

Her smile became truer. "Well, I feel like a total fool."

"Don't."

She wiped her cheeks again, trying to clear away any trace of tears that might remain. She didn't know it, but the tip of her nose was pink. He found that endearing.

"I should go," she said after a moment. "You will let me go now, won't you?"

"If you feel you have to."

She made no move to leave.

After a moment, she said, "I suppose I do blame my mother, just a little."

"As I said, it would only be natural."

"But I blame my grandfather more. He is not a nice man."

"There's nothing in any rule book that says a grandparent has to be nice. People are the same as they've always been. They've just collected a grandchild."

He chanced a smile, and she returned it, showing a quick flash of dimple. Her spirit was returning. Maybe one day, they would talk more about her mother and about the man who had hurt her. For a moment, though, this was enough.

She said, "Michael and I used to call him The Grinch, and it wasn't a compliment."

"You can imagine what my Aunt Minnie used to be called. But she doesn't look anything like a Disney mouse! Well, on second thought...."

Francesca laughed. Full dimple. It was all Randall could do to stay where he was.

"I'm curious about something," he said after a moment. "How did you come to have all those jobs? My God, what a background! Are there any left you didn't tell me about?"

"I had to work my way through school. Let's see— I've also worked for a dog-exercising service, a laundry, a bakery and once, a car dealership. That didn't last long, though. They didn't like it when I got some orders mixed up and a few people got the wrong cars."

He laughed. "Oh, Frankie!"

"You wouldn't have thought it funny if that had happened to you. No, wait, maybe you would. These were really exotic cars."

"I'll stick with my Civic."

She shook her head, pretending to feel sorry for him.

Randall was conscious that this was the first conversation they had ever had in which there was no feeling of strain. She had become more relaxed than he had ever seen her. He felt he was making progress. The world was good!

Then she said, "I really do have to go. Professor Brinkman needs some information tomorrow and I'm supposed to find it for him. And after what happened in the office earlier, I'm behind."

The moments had been short but very sweet.

Randall didn't hesitate. He wanted her to trust him. He wanted her to see that she could *always* trust him. "I'll take you back," he said.

THEIR CONVERSATION WAS comfortable as he drove her back to the school. The difference from the trip to his apartment was like night and day.

When he pulled into a space in the car park, she looked at him curiously. "You could have dropped me off," she said.

"I found you in the building, I'm taking you back there."

Her smile was rather bemused, but she accepted his company on the walk. "Have you heard?" she asked as they stepped into the hallway of her building. "Michael and Susan are setting a date. For a time, they thought about waiting until after Susan graduated. But now, they've decided not to. They just told me last night."

"Good idea."

"So you're not still opposed to the marriage?"

"Not at all. If Susan likes your brother, I like him."

Francesca looked pleased as she opened the door to her office.

Randall hovered in the doorway. He didn't want to leave, but he couldn't come up with a good excuse to stay.

She turned to look at him. "Thank you for helping us earlier. All those people were rather amazing. Sometimes, I find it a little hard to believe."

He shrugged. Where were all the words he wanted to say? He had to at least ask to see her again. Beg, if need be!

Always the master of the unexpected, Frankie planted a soft kiss on his cheek, then she stepped quickly away. She smiled at his shocked reaction.

"What was that for?" he asked.

"For being such a nice person. I'm sorry I was so nasty to you before."

Which before? he wondered, then decided it didn't matter.

"Frankie. . ." he began, his words husky.

She placed a finger over his lips. A smile was in her eyes. They seemed to glow, riveting him to the spot. His heart skipped a beat. She was so amazingly beautiful!

"Would you like to come over to my place tomorrow?" she asked. "Michael and Susan are stopping by for dinner. We're going to make spaghetti."

By now, Randall's heart was thundering. He had to work hard to keep it from leaping from his body.

Would he like to come? He'd like to see someone try to stop him!

"Sure. Yeah. I'd like that."

"Would you like my address?" she asked, still smiling.

Randall started. He'd forgotten! He had no idea where she lived!

"I'll write it down," she offered.

He stopped her. "Just tell me."

She gave the street name and apartment number.

"Got it," Randall said.

She shook her head, again bemused at his unusual talent.

"What time?" he asked.

"About six."

"I'll bring the wine."

"Great!"

Again, neither moved. Did she not want him to leave, either? Randall remembered the times before—years ago, it seemed—when she had responded to his kisses. Would she respond like that again? The temptation was almost more than he could bear.

By monumental force of will, he pulled himself away. "I'll be there," he said, starting to back up. He bumped against the door frame. "At six." He bumped into someone walking in the hall. After excusing himself, he looked apologetically at Frankie.

She stood in the doorway, her eyes laughing, a small, amused smile on her lips.

Randall waved and hurried away.

Slow and easy, he told himself. He had to take it slow and easy. Even if it meant he ended up in protective care!

SUSAN CAUGHT A RIDE to Frankie's place with Randall the next evening. Michael had an appointment with someone from the Masseys' publicity department and would be a little late.

This was the first time Randall and his sister had been completely alone since all the upset. Randall glanced at her a couple of times as they made their way to an area near the university. She looked different, more grown-up. Some of her features were still those of the little girl she once had been, but there was something else in her expression now, a new confidence, a new awareness.

She caught him looking at her and smiled. "I'm glad you could come tonight," she said.

"Why's that?" he asked, accelerating through an intersection when the light turned green.

"Because I've missed you. We haven't seen nearly enough of each other lately. You've been busy. I've been busy."

Randall smiled wryly. "Busy getting engaged."

She swiveled on the seat to face him, watching him as he drove. "I've been wanting to talk to you about that."

Randall lifted an eyebrow.

"We've set a date. Michael's birthday, October 1. I want you to walk me down the aisle," she explained.

"You do like Michael, don't you? Oh, please tell me that you do. It will mean so much to me if—"

"I like him."

She grinned happily, then sobered. "I was afraid you wouldn't because— Well, because he's different. I wouldn't have imagined myself with someone like him two years ago. I was so determined to get my degree. To find some quiet, unsuspecting little company and take it from being quiet and little to being huge and well-known. But that isn't what I want now, Randall. Everything in my life has changed. Can you understand that, even just a little?"

Randall acknowledged that he had a slight idea. She didn't know it, but he had been through quite a change himself. Quite a change.

Susan's smile reappeared. "Oh, I can't tell you what a relief that is! I thought you *wanted* me to get my masters in Business. You always encouraged me so strongly. And whenever I told you my plans, it was like they were your plans for me, too. That's why I couldn't tell you about Michael. I kept putting it off and putting it off. I didn't want to disappoint you!"

Randall found a parking place not far from Frankie's address and slipped into it. He cut the engine and turned to his sister, one arm draped comfortably on the steering wheel of the Civic, the other on the seat behind his sister's head. He gruffly tweaked her hair. "Disappoint me," he murmured. "I don't care whether you get an MBA or a CPA. An MD or a DDS. Or even a MRS. I want you to do what makes

you happy, Susie. I don't care about anything else."
He paused. "It bothered me that you didn't tell me
about Michael or about any of the rest. I hoped that
you wouldn't think I'd disapprove, because I don't.
I'm proud of you."

She looked at him with shining eyes. "Then you
don't care if I change my major? I know it will put me
behind, but I've learned so much about life, about
myself. I was so selfish before. Now, I'm trying not to
be." She studied him closely. "Something's different
with you, too, isn't it? Michael said he thought that...
But I didn't believe him. Now, I'm beginning to think
that maybe I was wrong."

Randall reached for the handle of the door. He was
unsettled enough in his own thoughts; on edge. He
didn't want his sister to try to dissect any part of his
deeper psyche. He braced himself against the cool-
ness of the evening, against the wind coming in off the
bay. He turned up the collar of his jacket.

Now it was his turn to receive speculative glances.
Finally Susan chose the direct approach. "Is it true?"
she asked. "Do you love Frankie?"

He tried to hide behind the collar.

"Do you?" she asked. "Do you really?"

Randall stopped. He turned to face her, weathering
the excitement in her expression.

"What if I do?" he questioned sharply.

"Then maybe we can have a double wedding!"

Randall snorted and continued to walk. Susan
skipped along at his side, not at all caring that some

might think she was much too adult for such a display. "How about Frankie?" she asked. "Does she love you? Have you told her? Has she told you?"

Randall slowed to another stop, shaking his head. "No one's told anyone anything. Well, hardly anything. It's all rather delicate at the moment."

"Oh," she said, disappointed. "That means you want me to keep quiet."

"I'd appreciate it. We have to go slow and easy. Tonight is just a beginning."

Susan began to smile again. "Frankie's not stupid. She'll know a good man when she sees one. I doubt it will take much time at all."

"Slow and easy," Randall cautioned. But he hoped that his sister was right.

Chapter Sixteen

One month later, during the intermission of the play *The Godchild*, Randall, Francesca, Paul and Allison were standing near the refreshments table in a crowded alcove. Conversations were abuzz around them. Everyone seemed happy and excited about the play. It had been well received over its extended run. In another week, the entire production would be moving to New York.

"Frank must be extremely pleased. Have you talked to him since the first performance?" Randall asked Allison.

"He's ecstatic. I don't think he believes it's really happening. He's waited so long to have it produced."

"He always claimed it was special," Paul said. "But no one believed him. It was hard to tell which was talking, him or the booze."

"He's doing a little better with that now," Allison said quickly to her husband. "He's trying."

Paul shrugged.

Francesca watched Paul's face. She could tell he wasn't wild about the man, but she wasn't sure why. She knew it had something to do with the time Paul and Allison first knew each other. Randall had told her that much, but he had given her no explanation.

It had taken a little while, but she was beginning to feel like a part of the group, the weeks in their company finally taking hold. She had liked Allison immediately, even on the first day she had met her, when she so desperately needed to find Randall to tell him of the meeting with Philip Massey. The sweetness of Allison's personality showed through. It was impossible not to like her.

Paul was another matter. He was extremely handsome and extremely hard to get to know. She had been put off by him at first. He could be so intense. But watching him with Allison, watching the way he cared for her, loved her, watching his banter with Randall and the deep trust the two men shared, she had come around.

Randall lightly squeezed her hand, drawing her gaze. He smiled at her and she smiled back, her heart fluttering in spite of her instructions for it not to.

"Are you enjoying yourself?" he asked, leaning close. There was a touch of anxiety in his gray eyes, as well as a tension she had sensed growing in him from day to day.

"Very much," she replied.

He looked so handsome standing there. Not at all threatening in his manner or in his looks, and his smile was wide and freely given.

"Would you like something to drink?" he asked.

"Yes, please."

He nudged Paul, and both men got in line at the refreshment table.

Allison looked beautiful in a soft pink dress with a string of pearls gracing her neck. With her red-gold hair, the dress's color might have clashed, but it didn't. In contrast, the look was stunning. She drew nearer to Francesca. Conversations still raged around them. Laughter tinkled in the air.

"I am enjoying the play," Francesca said. "And I'd say that even if I didn't know you knew the playwright."

"That's the way I feel, too. This is our second performance and it's only getting better. Frank is a very sensitive man. I think he's touched a nerve with a lot of people. People should be kinder to each other. Not so—"

"Afraid to love?" Francesca supplied.

"Exactly." Allison hesitated, then said, "I was afraid to love Paul at first. It's a complicated story, but there were many reasons why I shouldn't. One in particular. But I fell in love with him anyway. There wasn't anything I could do about it. Love has a way of happening like that. You might not want to, but you do."

Francesca returned her look. Allison wasn't talking only of herself and Paul; she was talking about the two of them as well. "He loves you, Frankie," Allison continued softly, making her meaning unmistakable. "If you love him, don't waste time. Don't make yourself wait. Don't make him wait. Not when there's no valid reason. But if you don't love him, don't hurt him. Don't lead him on."

At that moment, the men returned, each carrying two glasses and laughing at something that one of them had said. Their arrival effectively prevented any reply that Francesca might have made. Impulsively she reached for Allison's hand, pressing it, and the smile she gave was enough to light an answering smile in the face of her new friend.

RANDALL WALKED AT Frankie's side, extremely aware of everything about her. From the light perfume she wore to the delicate earrings that hung from each pierced ear. It was getting harder and harder as each day passed for him to keep firm control of his emotions. Still, he managed to hold himself in check, not wanting to push her in any way. He wanted to gain her trust.

Over the past month, they had gone to dinner, to movies and to the ballet. They had gone on picnics and on walks. And she hadn't told him to push off...yet. Neither had she let him know very much about her feelings. He thought he was making inroads, but he wasn't sure. They had had no deep talks again. Everything had been kept light and enjoyable.

But tonight, since seeing the play, she had been very quiet. Almost distracted. All too soon, they arrived at her door.

"Would you like to come in?" she asked, surprising him. She never asked him inside after one of their dates, and he had never pressed. The spaghetti dinner she had hosted for him and Susan and Michael had been his first and last time inside her home.

Once inside, she switched on lights and offered him a seat on the sofa. "Would you like something to drink?" she offered.

They had just come from having coffee with Paul and Allison. He didn't really want anything more, but again, he nodded.

Her apartment had surprised him the first time he had seen it. It was warm and comfortable and somewhat conservative, not at all as he had expected. Maybe he hadn't been able to put from his mind the punkish way she had been dressed at their first meeting, or any of the other costumes she had come up with later. *Or* his memories of more than one wild chase....

He looked up when she returned carrying two ice-filled glasses.

She sat on the couch a little way from him and sipped her glass of tea, watching him over the rim.

Randall moved uneasily under her perusal. He didn't know what to make of this evening. She had seemed happy enough at the beginning of it. The play was thought provoking, not sad, and its ending was upbeat, leaving the audience in a good mood. Had he said something to upset her? He racked his brain for a cause.

"I think that man in the play was silly," she said all of a sudden.

He shook all other thoughts from his mind. "In what way?" he asked.

"He should have told the child he was his father. Then there wouldn't have been all those complications."

"If he had, he'd have destroyed the boy's life."

"It ended up destroyed anyway... or almost destroyed."

"But he wasn't the one who destroyed it. He was the one who saved him."

"The child still didn't know that the man was his father."

"But he became his friend."

"Is being a friend enough?"

"In some circumstances. I thought you enjoyed the play."

"Oh, I did. I thought it was excellent. Frank Alexander is a talented man. And the actors who performed it were first-rate."

"But?"

"But I don't think being friends is a good idea sometimes. Take us, for example. You once said you loved me, and I said I didn't love you. We settled on being friends. Do you think that's a good thing to let go on for very long?"

Randall felt the blood drain from his face. She was telling him goodbye. In as nice a way as she could, she was telling him to get lost!

"Frankie," he said urgently, sitting forward. "We have to give this more time. One month isn't enough! I'll take some time off from work. Maybe we can go on a trip somewhere, not have any outside distractions—"

"I've always wanted to go to New Zealand."

"We'll go to New Zealand."

"I've heard it's a beautiful place for a honeymoon."

"Sheep. Lots of sheep. I know someone who went there last year. He said— What did you say?"

"I said I've heard it's a beautiful place for a honeymoon."

He looked at her in confusion. Did she mean what he thought she meant, or was he jumping to an awkward conclusion? Very carefully, he said, "A honeymoon . . . ?"

A slow smile touched her lips. "I refuse to be a kept woman. It's marriage or nothing!"

"But—"

"You don't want to marry me?"

Randall's heart skipped a beat. "Of course, I want to marry you!"

"Then . . . ?"

He still made no move to get closer to her. In fact, he was glued to the spot because he was afraid to breathe for fear the bubble of his dream might burst.

She put down her glass of tea and closed the distance between them. Then she tipped his chin back, touched his cheek in a soft caress and gave him a long, sweet, passionate kiss that told him this was no dream.

Randall didn't stay on the mark for longer than another second. Realizing his good fortune, he cradled her in his arms and drew her onto his lap. Then forgetting all prior restraint, he showed her why, from his point of view, it would be a very good idea for them to marry.

Finally, drawing back, he demanded, "You love me?"

"Yes!"

Randall felt intoxicated. "When did you decide that? Tonight? I thought you were acting strangely."

She shook her head "No, Randall, I've loved you for a long time. I even loved you when I told you that I didn't."

"Then why didn't you say it? Why did you put us both through this hell?"

"Because I was afraid."

The quiet admission pierced his soul. He had wanted her trust, and now, she had given it. He pulled her back into his arms, whispering, "Frankie... Frankie... You never have to be afraid like that again. I love you. I'll never hurt you. I'll never take advantage of you. Not ever!"

She clung to him, wiping ineffectively at the tears on her cheeks. "I know. But I was still afraid. It wasn't just you. I didn't want to love anyone! If you love someone, you become weak toward that person, vulnerable to what they say, to what they do. They can hurt you, hurt you badly. I'd already been through that once. Then there was my mother. Then Michael taking the tape—I was so afraid! Now it doesn't matter. None of it matters." She smoothed some strands of light brown hair away from his forehead. "I realized I loved you when those thugs broke into the house where Michael and Susan were staying. When I first saw them, I thought of you. I was afraid for *you*, afraid you'd be hurt. I didn't think about Michael until a second or two later. Then you did get hurt—"

"Not all that badly." He found her fingers and kissed the tips.

"I felt so guilty. I had dragged you into that mess without a second thought."

"I'd do it all over again to end up here."

She laughed. "Admit it. You thought you were a dead man more than once."

"Remind me never to let you drive the car when you're in a hurry."

"I even love the Civic!"

"Now I really know you care," he teased.

Her smile slowly faded. China blue eyes glowing with love took the moment to examine, with unaccustomed intimacy, the contours of his face. She found the tiny scar on his chin that had been caused by a childhood accident with a swing and the mark beside an eyebrow that was a legacy of chicken pox. Then her fingers fanned into his hair, threading lightly through the thickness beyond his temple before moving toward the back of his neck. Then she bent to touch his lips with hers, and she trembled.

It was all Randall could stand. He gathered her even closer into his arms and stood up.

"Which room?" he asked, his words husky.

She pointed to the left.

He found the bedroom unerringly.

"I love you," he whispered as he laid her down on the soft cover.

She was so breathtakingly beautiful, her pale hair so soft and fine, like silk. Her skin was a rich alabaster. Her eyes were two precious jewels. Randall couldn't believe that this was happening! Like a spark to dry gunpowder, she had exploded into his life, wrenching him from his everyday routine. She'd changed him, changed the way he looked at the world. Nothing would ever be the same again. She would be his most precious treasure for all the remaining days of his life.

Her hand lifted, reached for his and brought him down on the bed beside her. "This seems like a dream," she whispered, feeling the strangeness of his weight at her side.

"If it is, I don't ever want to wake up."

"Neither do I. Randall, I do love you. I don't want anything to ever happen to you. To us."

Randall thought of her father and of the little girl who had seen him go off to work one day, never to return.

He buried his face in the curve of her neck and kissed the sensitive skin. "I'm not planning to go anywhere. If you ever decide you don't like me, you're going to have one heck of a time getting rid of me. You've heard of Super Glue?"

She giggled. He enjoyed her laughter. Then their laughter stopped.

As the fog slowly crept over and around the hills of the city, creating a multitude of tiny cocoons in which existence went on as usual, in one of those cocoons, the joyous celebration of a new life together had begun.